A LADY'S PLAN

"I say, Miss Langston, you don't mean to confront Charles, do you?" Sir William asked anxiously.

"No, I don't think I shall let Charles know I am aware of his little secret," Audrey replied.

"But what are you going to do, Audrey?" asked Emmeline, watching as her cousin crossed the room and sat down at the delicate escritoire in the corner.

"I am sending a note to Madame Dufour, asking her to come tomorrow morning with new pattern books and fabric swatches."

"Whatever for?" asked Emmeline.

"I have my work cut out for me. Earlier I was ready to beg off the betrothal, but now I have decided to fight for Charles in every way I know how."

Emmeline chuckled, but Sir William still looked puzzled.

"And Madame Dufour?" he asked.

"New gowns, William. There is nothing better for a woman preparing to wage a battle," said Emmeline. To Audrey, she added, "New *daring* gowns!"

Books by Donna Bell

THE FIRST WALTZ
SWEET TRANQUILITY
BLUESTOCKING'S BEAU
AN IMPROPER PURSUIT
THE VALENTINE DAY'S BALL
A TASTE FOR LOVE

Published by Zebra Books

A TASTE
FOR LOVE

Donna Bell

Zebra Books
Kensington Publishing Corp.

http://www.zebrabooks.com

ZEBRA BOOKS are published by

Kensington Publishing Corp.
850 Third Avenue
New York, NY 10022

First Printing: January, 1999
10 9 8 7 6 5 4 3 2 1

Printed in the United States of America

One

"There are times, Will, when I think the deadliest evil of all is boredom."

"Surely not more deadly than old Boney's Guard, Charles."

"Yes, more than that. After all, I survived them, but I fear I'll never survive the life of an eligible bachelor during the Season in London. I mean, what's a fellow to do all day long?" Tall and slender, the Earl of Middlehurst shoved away from the table, his actions causing the servant to spring forward. The earl waved him away impatiently; he stretched out his long, muscular legs, crossing his hessian-clad ankles, an action that would have given his valet an apoplexy had he been in the elegant dining room. But it was only Charles's friend, Sir William Compton, who witnessed the earl's act of fashion sacrilege.

Sir William shook his head and observed, "Charles, you remind me of one of those new steam engines, ready to burst with pent-up activity. You've got to learn to relax and enjoy life. We've been home for almost a year. You should have the knack of acting the gentleman by now."

"And what is there to enjoy about this idle occupation of gentleman? How is one to pass the time, get through the day?" demanded Charles, shaking his head as a lock of blond hair fell across his forehead. He sat forward suddenly, his keen blue eyes fixing his friend with a fierce gaze.

Sir William, long inured to his companion's intensity, replied calmly, "Well, for one thing, he doesn't rise at dawn; he stays out till three or four in the morning and sleeps till noon, at the very least."

"A decadent lifestyle, to be sure," said Lord Middlehurst; he sat back again, his movements smooth and supple. Eyeing his friend with distaste, he added, "You have settled into it very well, I see."

"Mea culpa," came the reply. Sir William Compton snapped his fingers, and a footman hurried forward. "Give us another bottle of this brandy, Robbie. Oh, and a couple of cigars?" he said, one brow querying his friend.

Charles shook his head and sat forward, propping his elbows on the table's shiny surface and resting his chin on his hands. One slender finger tapped the side of his chiseled jaw.

"You could always go to Drake's tomb for the winter," suggested William.

"The deuce, you say. You must have forgotten that week we spent there before we left for Spain. We nearly froze to death in that dratted mausoleum, and it was June! No, I thank you, I'll stay here in London and perish of boredom. At least the town house has working fireplaces and chimneys that don't choke a fellow with smoke."

"So what are you going to do? About the boredom, I mean," said Sir William.

"Do?"

"Yes, do. I know you, too well, Charles. Whenever you get like this, it is only a matter of time before you hatch some scheme—usually something outrageous—to alleviate your intolerable ennui." A slow smile transformed his companion's face, and Sir William grinned in response. "Another donkey race?"

"Now, Will, this isn't Spain. Where in the world could we find any decent donkeys in London?"

"Well, it can't be another midnight raid on Wellington's cook's stash of chickens. And I don't think there are enough lizards in the park to get up a safari with our peashooters."

"No, no, nothing so trivial, to be sure. Besides, those amusements would only satisfy me for a short time. Then I'd be back in the suds again," said Charles.

"I know of nothing that can change your circumstances, old man. You're just doomed to be one of the pampered aristocracy. That's your lot in life," said William, taking a cigar from the box the servant brought to him.

"It doesn't have to be. If rank has its privileges, then I should be able to do as I please." Charles paused while the footman replenished their glasses; he then dismissed the servant and said quietly, "Do you remember how I enjoyed whipping up some dish out of nothing when we were near starving in Spain?"

"Yes, and bloody lucky I felt to be one of your entourage. Even when the rest of the regiment was half-starved, we ate well. Of course, I knew better than to ask what the ingredients of those tasty dishes were."

"Thank you. It was quite a challenge. But tell me, do you think I still have the touch? You have just finished one of my meals." Charles sat forward again, his face animated and eager. "What did you think of the boeuf diable?"

"You fixed dinner? I should have known when I couldn't identify the dishes. Much too elaborate, even for Gaston, your crazy chef."

"So you enjoyed everything?" asked Charles, his tone almost anxious.

"Delicious, absolutely delicious. Should I ask what was in each concoction?"

"Pheasant, ham, sweet potatoes, asparagus, and so on. Just the usual ingredients. But what I want to know, Will, is this: if you were going to dine at the club, would you consider this a meal worthy of your funds, worthy of comment, worthy of recommending to your friends?"

"Of course I would; I daresay I haven't had such a magnificent meal since leaving France. But what are you about, Charles? What are you planning?"

Charles Drake, Earl of Middlehurst, sat back again, his expression smug and thoughtful. "I believe I am going into trade, Will. I'm going to be a chef."

It was not an easy task to shock the unflappable Sir William Compton; having faced enemy charges without so much as a quiver, he was considered beyond astonishment. Now, however, he jumped to his feet and marched the length of the long, polished table before turning and fixing his friend with a speculative frown.

He shook his head and murmured, "Damn."

Middlehurst answered him with a grin, and Will returned to his place, gripping the back of the heavily carved chair and expelling a long, slow whistle. Staring down at his companion, Sir William demanded, "Are you mad, Charles? I mean, it simply isn't done! What will the Ton say? What will your family say?"

"Why should I care?"

"Perhaps because you have yet to inherit your grandmother's fortune to go along with that musty old estate you received when you reached your majority! She'll have you excommunicated from the family!"

"She'll never know."

"Now you are deluding yourself, my boy. Not know? The woman is practically a sorceress! She'll know. She knows everything that goes on in London, despite the fact that she hasn't set foot in the city for over thirty years! Didn't she hear about that duel you and I staged when we were home on leave three years ago? And what about that opera dancer?" Will's carefully coifed Brutus crop suffered irreparable damage as he ran his long fingers through the red curls.

Lord Middlehurst sat back with a confident smile and said, "But this time she'll never know! No one will! I've thought it all out. It will be our secret!"

"But the servants, they'll talk. They always do. And our friends—"

"I shan't tell them, well, only a chosen few, you dolt. And you said yourself the Ton doesn't rise before noon. No one will notice that I am never to be seen in the mornings and afternoons. They'll just assume I never rise before the moon. I won't actually be at the restaurant when the fashionable come to dine, unless I decide to join the other diners, and I will alert my employees not to distinguish me in any way."

"So you have your mind set on this madness?"

"Yes."

Sir William shook his head, but a spark of mischief began to light his green eyes, and he chuckled.

Charles cocked his head to one side. "You think I can't do it?"

"No, no. I have no doubt that you are capable of becoming the most renowned chef in all of London. Or perhaps the most infamous—when you are discovered. Because, mark my words, you will be discovered. What is the first thing that happens to an excellent chef?"

Charles shrugged his shoulders, and Sir William continued, "Someone tries to hire him away. I can see it now, Prinney comes to dine, demands an audience with the chef, and discovers a peer of the realm in the kitchen!"

"Oho! You rate my culinary abilities highly indeed."

"No doubt about that, old man," said William, "But you'll never manage the double life!"

"You think I cannot keep my identity a secret?"

"Not a whisper of a chance," said Sir William, sitting forward.

"Five thousand pounds says I can, but you must do nothing to expose me," said Charles.

"Devil a bit! As if I will need to."

"Then you accept?"

"I accept," said Sir William recording the wager in his betting book. "At the very least, you will make the coming Season entertaining."

"Both entertaining and flavorful," said Charles, lifting his glass of brandy for a toast.

"Father, how could you?"

"Wasn't easy, dear gel. 'S taken me the better part of twenty-four years!"

"Father!"

"Now, Audrey, you mustn't take on so. Your father was only trying to increase our consequence," said the mousy woman from her usual station in the corner.

"He's got a demmed unfortunate way of doing so!" snapped the tall beauty. She returned her eaglelike stare to her father who was nodding off in the huge easy chair by the fire. "Father!"

"Wha . . . ?" he managed, his eyes fluttering, his expression foolish.

"The least you could do is pay attention!" exclaimed Audrey, her thick blond tresses rippling across her shoulders as she tossed her head.

"Ach, my head hurts. Don't take on so. It's partially your fault. Your dowry was mostly intact until last year. If you had only accepted one of those other whelps that came sniffing around—"

"Mr. Langston!" protested his wife.

"Well, 's truth!" he barked hoarsely. "All that money on those Seasons, and she turned up her nose at every one of 'em. I told you then, madam, that we were wasting the ready; there she was with a perfectly acceptable arrangement already made."

"And you told me not to worry since I was already betrothed," said Audrey, her tone sounding lofty even in her own ears.

Her father, however, set his jaw stubbornly and snapped, "Throwing my own words back at me, are you? And what if the grand Earl of Middlehurst finds someone else. He certainly hasn't rushed to your side since returning from the war! Maybe he already has another in mind!"

"Ohhh!" intoned his daughter, frowning fiercely before striding out of the room.

Unmindful of the morning chill, Miss Audrey Langston sailed past the frail butler and out the front door. She made a sharp turn when she reached the drive and was soon engulfed in heavy timber. Her pace slowed, but she covered the distance quickly with her long strides. After twenty minutes, her cheeks flushed with the exercise and chilly autumn air, she left the trees behind. A few more paces and she stopped, closing her pale blue eyes briefly before opening them to survey the vista below.

The cold, gray stone of the house in the vale appeared doleful on the cloudy day. Even the autumn leaves were not proof against the pervading gloom. It gave the scene a still-life quality; the only motion was one thin trail of smoke from the kitchens climbing beyond the low-lying fog, reaching for the sky.

Audrey closed her eyes tightly and tried to envision the house on a summer day, the apple orchard in full bloom, the lawns green. She had always dreamed that one day they would be dotted with children, ponies, a loving mother and father.

She opened her eyes, pushing the long strands from her face. Finally she removed the blue ribbon and shook her head, long blond hair undulating like silken waves as it fell into place.

Rethreading the ribbon beneath and tying it on top, she shook her head and said matter-of-factly, "A loving mother, perhaps. As for Middlehurst . . ."

She sank to the cold earth, her thoughts turning inward. She was four and twenty, well past the age of marrying, but that had never been a consideration. There had always been Middlehurst and their childhood betrothal. She had never really supposed it would come to that; she'd always assumed one day someone would come along, sweep her off her feet . . .

But the years had passed quickly; the Seasons had come and gone. The town bronze she had achieved had begun to tarnish, and she was not looking forward to another Season, not that her parents could afford to give her another anyway.

Perhaps it was time to remind Middlehurst. She knew he had returned from the war last year; she followed the Society news in the London paper. Middlehurst, along with a number of other eligible bachelors had sold out at the same time; their entry into London Society had created quite a stir. Middle-hurst hadn't come to call, of course. Audrey frowned; perhaps he had forgotten their parents' promises.

"I heard what happened."

Audrey jumped at the intrusion into her thoughts, but she managed a weak smile and patted the ground in invitation. Her lively cousin, dressed in a dark green riding habit that appeared ready to burst at the seams, joined her, frowning fiercely.

"Wish I could do something to help, Audrey," she began before falling silent again.

Audrey patted Emmeline's gloved hand and said sensibly, "Unfortunately no one could have kept Papa from squandering my dowry."

"The bounder!" said the girl, her husky voice squeaking indignantly.

Audrey shook her head and squared her shoulders. "You mustn't think too badly of him. He meant all for the best, you know. It is just that he is not very wise about investments and such. He meant only to increase my dowry."

"But what now? Will he be forced to sell off part of the estate?"

"Certainly not, Emmeline. You mustn't worry that we are about to be cast out of our home! Besides, I know you would always find me an attic closet to keep a roof over my head," said Audrey dramatically.

"This is not the time for levity," Emmeline intoned severely, the stern expression sitting oddly on her usually sunny face. "I know your father is only my uncle by marriage, but if you wish, I will speak to him about this."

" 'Twould do no good, Emmeline. Besides, it is not as though we were penniless. He didn't lose our home, and that will still be mine one day. Meanwhile, I will simply have to marry."

Emmeline frowned, considering the matter. Having grown up with four adoring brothers, she could not imagine any male, even her havey-cavey uncle, being capable of such perfidy.

Finally, she said, "There is nothing for it. You will have to come to London with me."

"Oh, I couldn't," said Audrey hastily.

"Of course you can. You know I am to go again. Papa says if I don't settle on a husband this year, he's going to put me in a convent. So you see, I must go, and I would much prefer having you with me. Besides, I stayed with your family two Seasons ago."

"True, but it is still an expense. And it is simply unnecessary. You know Papa arranged a marriage for me years ago. Papa will no doubt write to Lord Middlehurst, and he will come down here to marry me."

"And if he doesn't?" asked Emmeline quietly. The two cousins shared a silent gaze before Emmeline said brightly, "Besides, you may not want to wed the man. After all, he was only nineteen, and you were . . ."

"Eleven," supplied Audrey.

"Yes, when you met him all those years ago. You may take him in dislike."

The thought that Audrey had no choice in the matter hung between them awkwardly. Emmeline maintained her smile; Audrey had often marveled at her cousin's optimistic nature. Nothing kept Emmeline down.

Finally Emmeline said firmly, "You never know what London may hold this year, Aude. There are many fish in that sea. You owe it to yourself to look them over one last time."

"But I must be realistic; no one will marry me without a dowry."

"But you said yourself you are heiress to this estate. Some men would consider that a very appealing dowry."

"Second sons and other desperate fellows," Audrey laughed, the biting sense of humor she usually kept under wraps breaking free.

"Nonsense, even if you were not beautiful and elegant, you are a wonderful companion and friend. Those are not traits to be taken lightly. There are many sensible men in London during the Season. They are not all rakes and rogues. You come with me. We will give Middlehurst a chance, of course, but if you can't like the man, then we'll find you someone more suitable," said Emmeline, her husky voice ringing with confidence.

"Perhaps," murmured Audrey, holding at bay the panicky realization that she would have to wed, that she now had no choice in the matter. But, she told herself firmly, it is time. She could no longer live under the same roof as her father; this latest infamy had dissolved the last shreds of respect she had for him.

Nodding slowly, Audrey forced a smile to her lips and said firmly, "Thank you, Emmeline. I would love to share your Season."

Emmeline stood up and stretched out her strong arms to pull Audrey to her feet. Then, looking up at her elegant cousin, she said heartily, "That's the spirit, Audrey. You and I shall take London by storm. The Earl of Middlehurst will find he has to fight his way to your side if he wishes to beg a dance!"

Audrey laughed out loud, the sound wrapping itself around them in the heavy air.

"Don't trouble yourself," she reassured Emmeline, her own confidence bolstered. "It is not as if I have never received any flattering offers; it is simply that none of them appealed to me. And I suppose I should be glad Father didn't force me to wed years ago."

Emmeline's eyes widened; she was appalled at the thought of such a thing coming to pass. The only daughter of five children, Emmeline was the darling of her father. She never doubted that her happiness was always of paramount importance to her sire.

Unable to keep silent, she whispered, "Surely he would never have you marry against your wishes?"

"Not precisely. And I have had two or three prospects who would have been excellent husbands, but . . . Well, the truth of the matter is, I have been waiting for the fairy-tale ending, for my Prince Charming," said Audrey, her color deepening. She was usually so sensible, one who kept both feet firmly planted on the ground. It was discomposing revealing just how foolishly romantic she really was.

The practical Emmeline cocked her head to one side, her mannish hat sitting even more oddly on her dark curls. "But Prince Charming does not exist," she said.

"No," said Audrey, her gaze gliding toward the sprawling, gray manor house. The sun had broken through the clouds, sending the fog scurrying away. She raised her face to its warmth, chasing away the megrims before turning and saying resolutely, "No, he doesn't, and now I must put that dream aside. If it comes to it, I'm certain Middlehurst and I can rub along fairly well together. And if not, I shall simply have to make do. Now, let's hurry home. When I checked this morning, Cook was baking apple tarts. She'll serve them up with our tea, I'll be bound."

"Well, some of them," said Emmeline, grinning guiltily.

"I should have known where you were this morning. You had better have left a few for me!"

That evening Audrey waited until her mother and cousin were comfortably settled in the drawing room before she returned to the dining room where her father sat sipping his port. He flashed her a wary expression when she dismissed their old butler and the footmen who were clearing the table.

Sitting back in his chair, Rupert Langston downed the dark liquid and poured another glass.

"Would you care to join me, child?" he asked, indicating the empty glass on the tray.

"No, Papa, I have no need of spirits to speak of what we must discuss."

"Very well," he said, watching with hooded eyes as

his daughter took the chair beside his. She was a beauty, in a cool sort of way. Her eyes were too pale to be called lively, but they were blue like her mother's, a soft blue which had always calmed him. Yet she was unlike her mother, for Audrey's pale gaze hid a rapier wit.

Smiling at her, he added, "You can't say anything to me I haven't already said to myself."

"Perhaps, Papa, but I must know how things stand. Emmeline has asked me to share her Season; I want to know if there will be enough for such an expedition."

"Of course there is. I would never deny—"

Audrey placed her hand on his arm, and he fell silent. "The truth, Papa, unvarnished, if you please."

He took a deep breath, another sip of port, and said evenly, "Things are worse than they have ever been. We shall be forced to let go most of the staff, and perhaps even sell off some of the land."

"Oh, Papa," was all Audrey could manage.

"As for a Season, child, that depends on its outcome," he said slowly, looking her in the eye.

"My only purpose for going is to wed," said Audrey softly. "I have no other choice."

He smiled and patted her hand. "You are a dear girl for not saying what I so richly deserve to hear. I know you are blaming me, and rightly so; still, Audrey, it is time you were wed. I'll write to Middlehurst tomorrow—"

"No!" she said, her eyes icy now.

"But, Audrey, I thought that's what you meant!"

"No, I meant I would *choose* a husband!"

"Nonsense, girl, not when you are already betrothed to Middlehurst!" said her sire, standing to glare down at her. "Besides, he's rich as Croesus, so they say!"

Audrey, as tall as her father, jumped up, her chin set stubbornly.

"I don't care how much he is worth. I do not consider that slip of paper a betrothal!"

"It is a binding agreement between his grandmother and me. He has no choice but to honor it."

"Nevertheless, I do not wish to honor it, and since you saw fit to fritter away my dowry, I feel no obligation to do as you say!"

"You shall!"

"I shall not!" she replied, their noses almost touching.

The door inched open; Audrey's mother slipped inside and said quietly, "Rupert, Audrey, please. The entire household can hear!"

Lowering her voice, Audrey played her trump card and said, "Papa, you owe me the chance to find a man I can care for, one who can care for me. If Middlehurst is that man, then so be it; if not, I shall choose my own husband."

Her father took a step back, his head bowed thoughtfully. Finally he nodded, looking up again. "Very well, daughter. You shall have the chance to choose for yourself. But if, at the end of the Season, you have not chosen, I shall call Middlehurst to heel, and you will have him without further ado. Agreed?"

Audrey smiled and manfully extended her hand.

"Agreed."

* * *

Christmas brought cold and snow to London, and the new year showed no signs of softening. The Earl of Middlehurst parried his grandmother's command that he put in an appearance at his ancestral home by claiming that the roads were impassable, thus allowing himself the pleasure of his freedom while he continued to pursue his outrageous plan to enter trade.

Charles's enthusiasm for his task was such that he didn't feel the cold or the damp of the sleet and snow. Sir William, however, loyally remaining in town to bear his friend company, threatened to have runners put on his racing curricle. The Thames looked more like the North Sea, he grumbled, some portions frozen over completely and others, where the ships entered the river, having miniature icebergs.

White's, however, on this early morning in January, was snug and warm, its hearths boasting roaring fires, its occupants fortified by a stout punch.

"Finally I have located the perfect setting for the restaurant, Will, and my solicitor has taken care of the purchase so that my name is not to be found on the deed," said Charles, his voice lowered to prevent any other members from eavesdropping. He leaned closer to the fireplace, extending his hands to the warmth.

"Bravo," managed William before yawning hugely. "But those are not the details which will sink you, Charles. I'll bide my time; when spring arrives—if it ever does—the Ton will ferret out the truth, without any help from me."

Charles laughed and shook his head, his blond hair, unfashionably long, glinting gold in the firelight.

"I shan't wait till spring. I have hired my sous-chef, a hard-working Frenchman, an émigré, who has managed over the past ten years to acquire a small inn near Richmond which somehow supports his family of eight."

"Eight? By Jove, he is French, isn't he?" commented Sir William, momentarily diverted from their original subject. "But can you trust the man, him being a Frenchie and all?"

"No fear of that," said Charles. "Besides, he hates Napoleon almost as much as you do. He left France after his first wife and brother were killed at the Massacre of Vendémiaire, and since old Boney was the eager, young general who ordered the execution, Rimbeau has no love for the little Corsican."

"Bravo for Rimbeau!"

"Shhh! I should warn you, William, there is also a daughter," said Will, his eyes glinting with mischief.

"Ah, that explains why you haven't been more forthcoming with your plans. Afraid I would—"

"Ruin everything by one of your misplaced, blundering infatuations," supplied Charles.

"Blundering?" intoned Sir William indignantly. "Should I remind you of the beautiful Angélica— Portugal's most beautiful flower?"

"Ha! Must you forever live in the past, the only

time in which your efforts were more successful than mine?"

"Then you admit it!" exclaimed William. "I knew you wanted the chit for yourself; she was a tasty little morsel."

Charles hastened to change the subject, not caring to hear anew his friend's boasts. He rose and brushed a crumb from his perfectly tailored coat of blue superfine. "Come along, I want to show you the site."

"Now? But it's snowing again!" protested William.

"So it is; then we had best go in my carriage. Why you will insist on driving yourself in that high-perch curricle, I'll never know! After all, there are no ladies in town to impress with your driving prowess."

"Just because I don't want to be seen slogging about in some cursed hearse—"

They stopped in front of an old inn, a huge, rambling structure which had never been completed. Charles handed the ribbons to his tiger and jumped down, looking about carefully before he unlocked the double doors. He motioned William inside and closed the doors after them.

"Well?"

"I believe it is colder in here than it is outside," said Sir William.

Charles strode past his friend and impatiently threw aside the tattered curtains on the far wall, letting the meager light filter through the dirty windowpanes.

"Come here," said Charles, his tones commanding.

William obliged and crossed to his side, shivering as he gazed out on the icy Thames. "Humph! I suppose it will be quite nice in the summer."

"Nice? Just imagine, if you will, Chinese lanterns lighting the lawn, the lights reflected on the water. Imagine the aroma of boeuf Bourguignon, the bouquet of a snifter of fine brandy, the delicate perfume of your lady love. Now what do you think?"

"I think I need a demmed better imagination to forget how deuced cold I am right at this moment," said William, holding up his hands when he looked at his friend's impatient blue eyes. "Very well, it should do nicely. But tell me one thing, you do plan to finish that wall over there, don't you? And what about the holes in the roof? I do believe I see snow falling in that corner."

"Of course, of course. I've only just signed the papers. I shall have the workmen begin as soon as the snow stops. The kitchen was never finished; I suppose that is when the original owners ran out of money."

"It is a good location. Not too far out of the way, but not in the midst of everything. Wouldn't do to have you coming and going on Bond Street or anywhere like that. But I say, could we please get back in the carriage before those hot bricks start collecting ice."

"Yes, of course. I guess it is rather cold in here. I'm too excited to feel the chill, I suppose."

They hurried back to their equipage. Charles took the ribbons and whipped up the single horse to a slow trot.

When they were comfortably ensconced in Middlehurst's library, Sir William said, "At least the Season won't be dull."

"No, not this one. I can hardly wait! All I need do is appear at the odd rout or ball, maybe Almack's once each month, and no one will be the wiser. Then, in the daytime, I can be at Chez Canard, cooking up each night's delicacies."

"Chez what?" asked Sir William.

"Canard," replied Charles, grinning.

"I say, isn't *canard* French for duck?"

"Yes, and what do you call a male duck?" He paused, watching his friend's brow wrinkle. "A drake, you dolt, as in Charles Drake, Earl of Middlehurst."

"Charles, you dog, you'll be your own undoing, scattering clues about for people to discover your identity."

"If a man can't amuse himself, then what good is it? And I am having the time of my life, Will."

"If you are not found out," said Sir William.

"Don't worry, I shan't be. This Season will be a complete success, a Season we'll never forget!"

Two

As the gray winter of 1817 settled over London like a woolen blanket, wrapping the city in a damp chill, Charles Drake, Earl of Middlehurst, continued to be unaffected by the atmosphere of gloom. He was, as his friend Sir William Compton grumpily observed, deuced annoying in his cheerfulness. But Charles's exalted mood persisted, keeping pace with each step toward the completion of his restaurant.

Each morning, attired in commoner's garments, he made his way to the river, inspecting the work performed the day before and reviewing with Rimbeau the work for that day. The kitchens would boast the most modern ovens; there would be an ice cellar deep below the ground floor. The chandeliers for the dining room were of the finest cut glass; the ceilings were plastered and then gilded. William, rising early one morning to accompany Middlehurst on his rounds, whistled in appreciation.

"Should have had that artist fellow, the one who's all the rage, paint a host of angels or cupids on the ceiling."

"I thought of it, but it hardly seemed appetizing.

So we settled on a bit of gold trim. Much more Tonish, don't you think?"

"Hmmm, I suppose so," said Sir William, strolling to the far windows just as he had on that cold day in December. This time, the scene that greeted him, though cold and gray, was one of order and elegance. Stone benches dotted the gently sloping lawn, and new shrubbery lined pebbled walkways.

Shaking his head in wonder, William said, "You know, Charles, I still think you'll be discovered straightaway, but I do believe you've got the right idea here. Why, I shouldn't be surprised if you don't make a go of the place, even if the Ton does discover you're the chef."

"If? Do I detect a lack of confidence about our little wager?"

"No, of course not, I merely meant to say it will be a shame when you are disgraced; this is shaping up to be a first-rate establishment."

"Thank you, William. Knowing how exacting you are when it comes, not only to dining, but to atmosphere, I am doubly complimented."

"So you should be. By the by, have you heard from that charming grandmother of yours lately?" asked William, his dark eyes twinkling merrily.

"I don't think she has recovered from my not coming to heel at Christmas. But that's all to the good. I don't need her interference now."

Wrapped in a soft blanket, Miss Audrey Langston huddled over the meager fire in her bedchamber.

When she had told her cousin Emmeline that they were not on the verge of losing their house, she had not known they were quite so close to being at a standstill. Although untitled, the Langston family was one of the oldest in England. Her father, the younger son, had inherited Langston Manor, an unentailed property which would one day pass to his only child on his death. Though he was an excellent estate manager, he had always dabbled in other investments, and never wisely. But this time it was worse than usual.

Her father had managed to keep the property intact, but they were in straitened circumstances. He had, however, set aside what remained of her dowry for the coming Season.

If there is really any of it left, thought Audrey, wondering if she should put the last log on the fire now or save it until morning. Not having enough firewood or candles made for very short days at Langston Hall. In the mornings, she stayed abed longer, snuggled under the counterpane. Even her cat, Euripides, crawled under the top blanket. Evenings ended early, too, no one wishing to converse over the tea tray when there was little to do except shiver in the cold drawing room.

In the end, Audrey opted for warmth at night and threw the last log on the flames, stirring up the embers to ensure the wood would burn evenly. This task accomplished, she tugged two bricks from the grate, wrapped them in flannel cloths, and scurried to the bed, her shoulders shivering under the wool blanket as she warmed the sheets. Then, diving under the counterpane, Audrey reached up to light the lone candle. Turning on her side, she opened the dog-eared novel Emmeline had given her for her twenty-fourth birthday last fall. She could almost recite the lines, but she savored each word, pausing here and there to picture the dark-haired hero as he rode *ventre à terre* to his sweetheart's side.

When the candle had burned down to the halfway point, she blew it out, tucking the book under her pillow and pulling the covers up to her nose. Resolutely, Audrey closed her eyes and willed herself to sleep. Euripides moved up to her chest, his head resting on her arm.

Morning dawned bright and cold; Audrey was awakened by sharp claws kneading her skin. Impatiently, she turned over, trying to ignore the insistent meows of her friend. Finally, she threw back the covers, with Euripides leaping aside as she scampered to her door, setting the cat free.

Audrey returned to the bed long enough to fetch her blanket, wrap it tightly around her tall, willowy form, and search out her slippers. This done, she made her way down to the kitchens where she knew a decent fire and a hot cup of coffee awaited her.

"Good morning, Mrs. Hopkins, how is your arthritis this morning?"

"Better, thank you, miss; I think that sheet of copper under the mattress is going to do the trick."

"Good, but you must also remember to get out of this kitchen a little more. It does you no good to stay cooped up in here all the day long."

"I know, miss. Lord bless you, I know. It's kind you are to look after us like you do."

"Nonsense. One looks after one's family."

The rosy-cheeked cook beamed, her many chins resembling the bellows as she vigorously nodded her head. "That's just what Mr. Hopkins and I were saying th' other evening. You are the dearest child; we're going to miss you sorely when you go up to London."

Audrey smiled, and said quietly, "And I shall miss all of you."

Mrs. Hopkins patted her mistress's shoulder awkwardly. "Now then, miss, you mustn't be sad about going up to London. Why, it's happy you should be to be thinkin' of setting up your own household. That's what a woman is for, you know; that's what will make you feel complete. And before long . . . Well, you'll be ever so happy; I know you will."

"Thank you, Mrs. Hopkins. I'm sure I shall. And I am looking forward to this spring; at least we will all be warm again!"

"Aye, 'tis a cold winter we'll be having, you mark my words. We'll all be glad to see the last of it!"

"Yes, as far as I'm concerned, spring can't come soon enough."

Audrey made her way back to her room. She glanced out the windows and sighed. The sunshine that had greeted her when she awoke was losing its battle against a new wave of clouds; it would be gloomy again today. Nevertheless, she had promised the vicar's wife that she would accompany her on the parish visits, so she began to undress.

The pot of water she had left by the fire was warm,

but it chilled immediately as she sponged it over her body. Finally, shivering, Audrey drew on her woolen stockings and warmest gown. She took out her best wool pelisse, her fingers brushing with longing against her other pelisse with its fur-lining, so soft and cozy. Audrey shook her head; it wouldn't do to visit the sick and indigent wearing such a fine garment. It was only fit for London where she had purchased it two years before.

Leaving her room and making her way to the stables, Audrey passed no one. Their household, which had once boasted as many as twenty servants, was reduced to only five. In the stables were Mr. Hopkins and his son, the one stable boy. Of course, they now had only five horses to tend to, so any more servants there would have been ridiculous.

Pete pulled his forelock and hurried to harness her mare to the dog cart. The boy smiled at her, nodding when she greeted him, but he had never spoken a word to anyone. He was good with horses, though, and very obliging.

Away from the house, a frowning Audrey conversed casually with her mare, an eighteen-year-old bay, that had been quite spirited when she was younger. Now, though she still kicked up her heels occasionally, she was quite content to trot along the rutted roads, pulling the light cart.

"Only two more months, Cleo, and we'll be in London. You mustn't worry that Uncle Gilly won't let you come along with me; you know the whole family is horse-mad."

The pounding of hooves made Audrey guide her

horse to one side of the road and pull back on the reins. A moment later a loud halloo rose above the noise of hooves as the squire's son flew past. When the noise had faded, Audrey picked up the reins, and they continued to plod along.

"One of these days, Cleo, that young man is going to come a cropper. I only hope he doesn't break his neck—or someone else's. Still, what can one expect of youth?" she asked conversationally. Cleo shook her head and snorted. Chuckling, Audrey said, "Exactly. Young people are not what they used to be. Why, I would never have acted in such a manner. And neither would any of the young men of my acquaintance," she added, not bothering to mention that her knowledge of young men had been sorely limited until her first Season in London.

"You remember Middlehurst," she said to the mare. "Remember his visit the summer I was eleven? He was quite the young gentleman; a bit wild, perhaps, but never outrageous."

Audrey grew silent, trying to picture how that brash, spotted, nineteen-year-old boy might have turned out. He had had blond hair then; of course, that might have changed. He had been quite tall and had sat his horse well. Leave it to a young girl to remember such inconsequential details, she thought.

She frowned, trying to remember. Had he liked to play cards? Had he been talkative? Did he like to read? She couldn't recall any of the important details.

Then Audrey laughed out loud and commented, "I do remember what a wild ride we had when Charles had gone. Don't you, Cleo?" she asked the unresponsive mare. "Papa and Momma joyfully informed me that he would one day be my husband. I vowed I would not wed at all rather than marry him. It's funny now; I don't remember why I should have taken him in such dislike."

To herself, she said quietly, "But I do hope he has changed."

She guided the cart into the yard of the vicarage and hopped down.

"Good morning, Mrs. Crenshaw," she called when a gray-haired woman, her arms full of baskets, appeared. "Let me help you," said Audrey.

"No, no, I can manage, but there are more in the kitchen. If you would be so kind . . ."

With the cart loaded to capacity, the two women set out for their first destination, the Thomas family.

"Good morning, Mrs. Thomas. How are you and that new baby doing?" asked the vicar's wife, climbing down awkwardly.

Audrey marveled at the spry manner in which Mrs. Thomas moved to greet them. No one would guess she had only given birth a week before.

"We're fine, Mrs. Crenshaw. Come inside and see the little one. Good morning, Miss Langston," she said with a quick curtsy.

After they had admired the latest addition to the Thomas household, Mrs. Thomas asked timidly, "I do hear you're going up to London this spring, Miss Langston."

"Yes, I think it is high time I settle down."

Mrs. Thomas and Mrs. Crenshaw exchanged nods.

"It's what every woman wants—a home, a husband,

and children," said the woman, smiling down at the baby at her breast.

"How are the rest of your offspring?" asked Audrey. "And Mr. Thomas?"

"We're fine, miss; don't you fret about that. My James would never let us starve. We're doing just fine, and all the children are hardy, too. I only asked about London because . . ."

Audrey hastened to reassure Mrs. Thomas that she had taken no offense, but the knowledge that James Thomas had, until just recently, worked as the head gardener at Langston Manor hung awkwardly between them.

As the morning wore on, time and again, Audrey was counseled and questioned about her coming visit to London. It was obvious that her marriage was not just of passing interest in the neighborhood; for many of them, her marriage would mean the return of prosperity to their own lives.

Crawling into her bed that evening, Audrey couldn't help but say a little prayer that she find someone, and quickly. As the lone candle flickered and went out, she thought perhaps her betrothal to Middlehurst was no bad thing. It could turn out to be very convenient for many people.

January turned to February, and Charles continued in his sunny mood. He spent hours planning menus and testing new recipes on his friend William, who grew annoyed at being interrogated on each spice, each ingredient.

Finally, Sir William had put up with enough and complained, "Devil take you, Charles, I don't give a damn whether the rosemary suits the blasted lamb. You are driving me mad with all this analyzing; you are a master chef, I grant you, but give over or I shan't so much as set foot inside your blasted establishment!"

"I'm only . . ." the Earl laughed.

"Devil take you, Charles. This winter has been interminable. First of all, you wouldn't leave London. For pity's sake, three-quarters of Society have retreated to their country homes to wait out this ghastly weather; the others venture out only when absolutely necessary, or when they can no longer bear the company of their families. You, however, are up every morning at dawn, gallivanting here and there, kitted out, I must tell you, in the most abominable fashion. Why, when old Pomfret told me he thought he had seen Middlehurst in servant's garb, I had to lie, Charles, simply lie."

Smiling with the most deplorable lack of concern for his friend's sensibilities, the earl asked, "What did you tell him?"

"That your father—wink, wink—was a regular Don Juan with the ladies, and that he had no doubt seen one of your natural siblings."

"My father was practically a monk," protested Charles, his lips twitching irrepressibly.

"Oh, everyone thinks that about his father; I daresay your sire was as spirited as the next fellow in his day. Anyway, old Pomfret seemed to have no trouble believing he had seen your father's by-blow. Might be something to that . . ." added William, his thoughts diverted.

"Nevertheless, Will, I appreciate your looking after my reputation, especially since you could so easily have won the bet if you had encouraged Pomfret in his suspicions."

"Yes, well, I didn't think of that in time, or I would have been sorely tempted. But dash it all, Charles, you've got to quit being so careless. I mean, Pomfret is a doddering old man, and he saw you. What if someone like Asherton or Dillingham were to be coming home from a late night at the club and were to run into you?"

"If they had been there all night, I daresay they would be too drunk to recognize me, but I will try to be more circumspect."

"And for God's sake, stop being so demmed happy all the time. That alone, considering the weather, is enough to make you suspect," grumbled William.

" 'Fraid I can't help that, old man. I am happy. I have finally reached an agreement with Rimbeau. He really didn't want to uproot his family and move them into town, but I persuaded him to leave them in Richmond and come to town himself. And his daughter Colette, of course."

"Ah, yes, the divine Colette."

"Forget about her; you'd make ten of her. She is just a child; hits me about here," he added, indicating his waist.

"How old did you say she was?" asked William.

"Twenty, but she will have none of you."

"So you say, but my charm, you know, has toppled many a maiden."

The light of laughter died in Charles's eyes, and he said sharply, "Never mind about Colette. The last thing I need is for my sous-chef's daughter to fall under your spell. I need her to work, not daydream, be she ever so beautiful."

"Aha! So you admit she is beautiful!"

"I suppose so; I really haven't thought about it. I've been much too preoccupied with the restaurant."

"And when will you open?"

"The second week of March. That will give us a chance to have everything operating smoothly before the Season really gets under way. I am counting on you to bring your aunt Kathryn shortly after we open."

"The devil you say!" exclaimed Sir William, sitting up straight and tugging at his cravat to give himself more breathing room. The thought of his aunt was always enough to make him uncomfortable. "I think that's asking a bit much, Charles. The woman's a regular tartar. Don't wish to be disobliging, but—"

"But nothing. Some other night, you can bring a few of the fellows from the club, but that won't insure the patronage of the females of the haut Ton. I want all of them to know that Chez Canard is the most tonish of the Ton, so that all of them will be fighting for a table by the time the Season truly begins. Just wait and see!"

"Oh, very well. I suppose I should help bring you into fashion; the more people who visit this restaurant of yours, the sooner I'll win my bet!"

* * *

"But, Rimbeau, I was counting on you!" exclaimed Charles, striding about the dark-paneled office.

"Nevertheless, my lord, I cannot be the one to greet your guests. How would I look in my soiled apron, showing the aristocracy to their tables?"

Charles paused in his circuitous route, staring at his sous-chef without really seeing him. In the past two months, he had come to rely on this Frenchman.

"Then what do you suggest, my friend?"

"I suggest you allow Colette to deal with our patrons," said Rimbeau.

"Colette? Why, she's just a slip of a girl."

"Humph! She knows how to handle the quality. She has a way about her."

Charles frowned, trying to envision the pert Colette handling the likes of the dashing Lords Asherton and Dillingham.

"You remember how handily she dispatched the attentions of your friend Sir William, and he even left with a smile on his face," said Rimbeau.

"True, true. I suppose she could do it. Do you think she would be willing? I mean, we agreed she would do the marketing and keep the books, but this—"

"She would be grateful. It would mean no more peeling potatoes or stirring sauces. She hates the kitchen."

"Very well, but I will ask, just to be certain. Would you send her in, please?" said Charles.

"*Certainement,* my lord."

"Rimbeau, no more of that. I am plain Mr. Brown now."

"Of course, forgive me, my . . ." Catching himself, the Frenchman bowed and left the room.

Charles sat down at the battered desk. It was huge, much bigger than he needed, but it served. When he had sent Rimbeau to find furnishings for the office, he had insisted on everything being plain. If anyone of his station did manage to penetrate the kitchens and reach this office, the earl didn't want it to display the richness of the aristocracy. It needed, instead, to be utilitarian and comfortable. Charles shifted uncomfortably on his chair. Perhaps, he thought, he had gone too far with the hard wooden chair. Surely a well-to-do restaurateur would have a soft leather chair at his desk. He would have to look into the matter.

"You wished to see me, Mr. Brown?"

"What? Oh, yes, Colette. Won't you be seated?" he said, rising briefly upon her entrance. Rimbeau was the only worker who knew Charles's true identity, but he thought the sharp-minded Colette had guessed he was more than a mere wealthy merchant.

"I have been discussing with your father the matter of who should manage the dining room, see to it that the guests are comfortable, and so forth."

He paused, his eyes flashing briefly on her breasts rising and falling rhythmically. Clearing his throat, he continued, "As you know, I don't wish to be actively involved in that aspect of the business, and your father has persuaded me that he, too, would not be a good choice. As a matter of fact, he has suggested that you might be the best person for these tasks."

"I?" she exclaimed, her dark eyes round with feigned surprise.

Charles found himself drawing in a quick breath of admiration; did she have any idea how seductive she looked with those dark eyes and her long, black hair twisted into a tight knot on the top of her head. She was a tiny thing, not more than five feet tall, but she had curves in abundance. He had been too busy over the past months to take much notice of the girl.

"Mr. Brown?" she said, breaking through his lascivious thoughts with a slight curve of her full lips.

"What? Oh, yes. Well, what do you think? Do you think you could handle the venturous bucks and the condescending ladies whom we hope will patronize our establishment?"

"Of course, Mr. Brown. I welcome the chance to be of service to you. But surely you will come out to greet the diners when they wish to compliment the chef?" she asked, regarding him intently.

"No, no. I shall leave that to your father. I want no glory. I simply enjoy cooking."

"And that is why dinner at Chez Canard will soon be the most sought-after meal in all of London," she said, standing up and shaking his hand. Then she was gone.

Charles stared after her. Then, looking down, he was surprised to see his hand still extended; he let it drop awkwardly to his side. What was it about the girl that totally unnerved him? She was so self-assured, so composed. He had never met another female like her, except perhaps his grandmother . . . Or that aging courtesan who had taught him the ways of love.

Charles laughed. He would have to tell William about the comparison. William had tried his luck with the beautiful Colette, waylaying her on her trip to the market so she would not connect him and the earl. Colette had repulsed his advances neatly without causing William any feelings of discomfort or embarrassment. But, as William had told Charles, he would never approach Colette again.

Yes, thought Charles, she would do very well as his maître d', or perhaps the term was maîtresse d'—mistress.

He laughed at this absurdity, his heart light despite the trepidation he felt about the opening of Chez Canard the next day. Tomorrow was the day he had been planning for, waiting for; nothing could possibly go wrong.

He had persuaded William to bring his pretentious aunt Kathryn. Charles would not join them, lest his presence make his workers nervous. He had not had many dealings with the waiters; he had given all his instructions via Rimbeau. But they knew him by sight and had been directed never to speak to him or single him out in any way. They knew he must be *somebody*, but they had no idea their master chef was a peer of the realm.

The restaurant was quiet when he left the office; everyone else had gone home for the evening. Upstairs, Rimbeau and Colette had retired. It would be some time before any of them would have another carefree night.

With a whistle, Charles slipped out the door, locking up before hailing the unexceptional cab he had purchased for his comings and goings from the restaurant. Seeing a hansom waiting outside a restaurant wouldn't cause any comment; none of the diners would ever know the cab was there every single day. Nor would they know it carried the mysterious chef who owned and operated Chez Canard.

"Take me home, Handie."

"Aye, sir," said the old servant. "Tomorrow night be th' night, my . . . sir?"

"Yes, tomorrow night will be the test."

"That's all right then, I been samplin' some o' the fare. Right good it is, even if it does taste a bit foreign-like."

"Thank you, Handie. I count that as a high compliment. Let's hope the people who come here tomorrow night are as complimentary."

"Are you sure you want to serve the mushroom fricasee, sir?"

"And why wouldn't I?" demanded Charles, glancing over his shoulder to scowl at Rimbeau. The Frenchman shrugged, a sure sign he was washing his hands of all responsibility where the mushroom dish was concerned.

"What's wrong with the mushrooms?" Charles pressed, turning over his spoon to a worker.

"There is nothing wrong with the mushrooms, sir," said Colette, entering the kitchens in time to hear her father's complaint. "I bought them myself. Do you think I would buy poisoned mushrooms?" she snapped, her dark eyes flashing angrily back and forth between the two men.

"No!" they said simultaneously.

"But the cream, my dear . . . I am afraid the cream has curdled. Turnley did not stir it properly," said Rimbeau, directing an accusing stare at the trembling cook.

Charles looked into the pan, closing his eyes briefly at the disaster he found there, and said crisply, "Have we any more mushrooms?"

"Of course, Mr. Brown," said Colette, marveling at the man's self-control. She would have shot Turnley or, at the very least, have sent him packing.

"You see, Turnley, you must get the mushrooms cooked to perfection before adding the cream. It is meant to be a sauce, added when the mushrooms are already finished cooking. You want only to warm the cream and eggs like so," said Charles.

"I'm ever so sorry, sir," said Turnley.

Charles turned the spoon over to the younger man and patted his back. He returned to the gravy for the braised pheasant, adding in the truffles and sweet-meat. He glanced around just in time to stop Turnley from committing another faux pas.

"Never add the lemon juice to the cream until you are ready to serve the dish!" he cautioned sharply.

"Yes, sir. I mean, no, sir."

"Let me finish it," said Rimbeau, taking over. "Turnley, you will come in early tomorrow morning for another private lesson, yes?"

"Yes, sir, Mr. Rimbeau. Thank you, sir."

Standing by his side, Rimbeau leaned toward the earl and whispered, "You should go now, my lord. Everything will be fine. We can manage."

"I know, Rimbeau, but it is very difficult not being here for the entire evening. I am finding this arrangement most unsatisfactory."

"But so it must be. And you must go home to change. You can hardly appear with your friends in your present state."

"I have been thinking about that. Perhaps I could leave some evening clothes here at the restaurant so I could change more quickly."

"Perhaps, but you must be very careful."

"I will. For now, I will bid you good night."

"Good night, Mr. Brown," said Rimbeau, beckoning to Turnley to return and take over the stirring.

"And, Turnley, always stir in the same direction," said Charles before he ducked out the back door.

Strolling away from the restaurant, he climbed into the cab, signaling Handie to take him home with a yawn and a wave.

The restaurant was a demanding mistress. They had been serving for only three weeks, but it was already so popular, they turned people away each night. He was spending much more time there than he had originally planned, but what was a concerned chef to do?

Still, tonight should help put to rest any rumors about him becoming a hermit or being ill. He had accepted invitations to three different entertainments. He would be thoroughly exhausted when he finally sought his bed. And rising to go to the restaurant in the morning would be agonizing, he thought.

The cab stopped in the alley behind his town house; with a groan, Charles hopped down and headed toward the blazing lights. Hurrying up the back stairs, he slipped into his bedchamber. Higgins, his exacting valet, "Tsked, tsked," as he removed Charles's stained shirt.

"Your bath, my lord," said Higgins, after pouring in another pitcher of hot water. His nose in the air, he removed the soiled garments from the room.

Charles sank into the warm water with a sigh, allowing his muscles to relax. The first evening he had made plans to go out after working all day at the restaurant, he hadn't taken the time to refresh himself with a full bath; he had paid for it dearly, feeling completely worn out as he suffered through a rout and a ball. Now, he knew better; the twenty-minute soak would make all the difference. Still, as he rose and dried himself, he eyed his comfortable bed with longing. This double life was taking its toll.

Charles dressed hurriedly in evening clothes and dancing shoes.

"What? Not ready yet? Step it up, old man!" called Sir William, walking in as the footman hurriedly announced his arrival.

"Almost there. Have had to start over twice on this blasted cravat. I tell you, Will, the working class have the right idea—keep it simple. Blast!"

Higgins produced another crisp white length of cloth, favoring Sir William with a look that dared him to interrupt this all-important task again.

"Yes, that should do," said Charles. Higgins nodded his approval, and they were off.

"Where are we going first?" asked Charles when they reached the street.

"The Garrisons' ball. We can get the dancing out of the way first. Wouldn't do for you to fall asleep doing the pretty to some eager miss. Afterward, we'll go to that deuced musicale, and finally, the Hendricks' card party."

"And where are we meeting Parnell and Asherton?"

"At the ball."

"Don't suppose we could talk them into a quiet night of cards at my house?" said Charles hopefully.

"Probably, but that could hardly be considered evidence that you are a normal, eligible bachelor enjoying a night on the town. Of course," added William thoughtfully, "from my point of view, that would be all to the good, eh? Bring a bit more suspicion down on the head of the mysteriously reclusive Earl of Middlehurst."

"All right, all right. But I shan't enjoy myself," snapped Charles.

"You will appear to be enjoying yourself, however. That is the important part," said William.

The evening went as planned, except that the card party proved to be a tedious affair with stakes so low they left after playing only two hands.

" 'Tis early yet," said Asherton, consulting his pocket watch.

"Too early to call it a night," William agreed, grinning at Charles who was stifling a huge yawn. Charles glowered at his friend.

"I, for one, am famished," said Phillip Parnell, a thin, reedy fellow who had always been impossible to fill up. In Spain, his appetite had been legend.

"What? Still hungry after that fine buffet at the Perrymans' musicale?" said Charles, disliking the gleam of deviltry in William's eyes.

"That was ages ago," complained Phillip.

"Absolutely ages," agreed William. "I say, have any of you dined at that new place? What's it called? Chez something. Took my aunt Kathryn and sister last week. Quite passable fare." William laughed out loud as Charles's jaw clenched and his eyes narrowed.

"I tried it," said Asherton. "Chez Canard, it's called. Quite good, actually."

"Well, where is it? Not far, I hope," said Phillip.

"No, not far at all," said Charles.

Whatever fears Charles held about appearing at his own restaurant were quickly put to rest. Colette seated them in a secluded corner, carefully avoiding any eye contact with him. She assigned the very best waiter to their table; McCoy served them quietly and efficiently without a hint of recognition. Charles wondered if he ever truly looked at the diners, except that he was always there to fulfill even the smallest request.

Two hours later, they had settled the bill and were once again on their way. Charles beamed with delight as Parnell patted his stomach and declared, "Even I am full after that meal. Must tell m' mother about the place."

Phillip Parnell, of course, was not a true test of the quality of the restaurant's offerings; he would eat anything, and was satisfied by quantity rather than quality.

Asherton, however, was another matter entirely. He considered himself a gourmet, very exacting in his culinary expectations.

Charles's smile broadened, and he favored William with a wink, as Asherton announced, "I must agree with you, Parnell. That was the best meal I've had since . . . why, since you cooked up that wild pheasant in Paris last year, Charles. In fact, several of the dishes put me in mind of those days. Must make it a point to go back to Chez Canard often."

"Yes, we must," said Sir William, clapping an elated Charles on the back as they strolled away from the restaurant.

Three

"Are you certain you remembered everything, dear?"

"Yes, Momma. Now, you will remember to take your tonic every day, won't you?"

"I'm sure Annie will remind me," replied Mrs. Langston, peering into the near-empty wardrobe. "Your uncle has kindly offered to supply all your gowns, Audrey. I don't know why you insist on taking all the old ones from last time."

"Because there is absolutely nothing wrong with any of them, Momma, and no one will remember them. After all, I didn't go last spring," said Audrey, taking her mother's hand and patting it, trying to remind herself to keep her impatience in check.

Being such a sensible girl, Audrey had found it very difficult growing up with a mother who was so vague about everything. But she knew her mother cared for her, which was more than many a young lady could say, so she tried to be patient.

"I have asked Mrs. Hopkins to remind Annie about your medicine, too," said Audrey, "so you should be fine."

"You are such a dear child. I will miss you." Her mother, standing on tiptoe, kissed Audrey's cheek. With love in her eyes, she smoothed her daughter's pale blond hair and straightened the bow of Audrey's serviceable bonnet.

"Time to go, miss," said Purser, their ancient butler.

Audrey nodded and kissed her mother's cheek before scooping up a bag of needlework. With a lightness in her heart, she made her way down to the traveling carriage her uncle had sent for her.

Her father waited beside it, his mouth quirked into that slight smile she had learned to distrust. He took her hands in his and kissed her lightly on both cheeks. Then, with a wink, he placed a heavy purse in her hands.

"What is this, Papa?" she asked, frowning as she tested its weight.

"You didn't think I would allow you to go to your uncle Gilbert as a beggar, did you? Why do you think we've been living like paupers, eh? Now, my girl, when you reach your uncle's house, you give that over to him for safekeeping. It should be enough to buy you any baubles you may take a fancy to."

"Papa, do you mean penny-pinching all this time, getting rid of all our servants, was just to save money for my Season? How could you!" she hissed.

"Shhh, now I won't hear a word of thanks. It's the least I could do for you, my dear," He helped her into the carriage and closed the door. Leaning closer, he said blithely, "The most I could do was write to Middlehurst and apprise him of your arrival."

"Papa!"

"Spring 'em, Cal! Good-bye, my girl!" he shouted as the horses leapt forward.

Hanging out the window, Audrey favored her father with an expression of outrage, but he was laughing too hard to notice.

For the next two hours, all the way to her uncle's house, Audrey wondered what her father's letter might have said. His only purpose would have been to remind Middlehurst about their betrothal. *How could he!*

By the time Audrey had alighted from the carriage and had received hugs from everyone, she was in a rare state. Sparing only minutes for the niceties, she excused herself, pulling Emmeline after her and up the stairs to the bright, warm room she always occupied when she visited her aunt and uncle.

"What is it?" exclaimed Emmeline when the door was closed.

"That is what I like about you, Emmie, you understand exactly what I am thinking," said Audrey, her tone tight with suppressed anger.

"You don't look as though you like anyone at the moment. I have never seen you so agitated," said Emmeline, her husky tones sounding odd with her whispering.

"As I left, just as I left, Papa told me he had written to Middlehurst to tell him about my visit."

"To Middlehurst?" gasped Emmeline. "But you wrote that he had promised to allow you to look about you for a husband to your liking."

"So he did," said Audrey, her blue eyes snapping

with ice. "But I suppose he doesn't think I can attract a husband on my own; he believes he must help me."

"Oh, Audrey, that is so unfair!"

"It's monstrous! And I shall write and tell him so!"

The dressing bell rang, and Audrey moved immediately to the dressing table and poured some water into the basin. It was still hot, a luxury she had grown unaccustomed to. Tears filled her eyes, threatening to spill over.

She wanted to tell Emmeline about her father's perfidy—all those loyal servants, dismissed for the sake of saving their wages for her Season—but she could not voice her outrage. She was too embarrassed to tell anyone of his baseness.

Audrey squared her shoulders and lifted her chin. "I shall show him!" she whispered vehemently.

Emmeline, who had wandered over to the fireplace, gave a low, guttural laugh.

Audrey spun around, frowning at her petite cousin.

Emmeline lifted her hand to cover her mirth. Composing herself, she said, "I'm sorry, Aude, it is just that you are usually so calm and levelheaded; Papa counts on you to pull me out of scrapes. Perhaps this Season I shall be the paragon of virtues."

At this unlikely description, both girls fell into whoops. The dinner bell sounded before they had regained their equanimity.

Descending the stairs, Audrey confided, "At the very least, just to spite my father, I shall try to take Middlehurst in dislike!"

* * *

The carriage rolled to a stop, and the door flew open before the footman could reach it. Emmeline jumped to the ground, staggered away, and fell to her knees. Audrey, only steps behind, put her hand on her cousin's shoulder and waited helplessly for the retching to cease.

She helped Emmeline rise and led her back to the carriage.

"Perhaps you should let Riggs give you a dose of laudanum," said Audrey.

"No, I hate giving in to it," moaned the girl.

"Then let's go."

"Really, Audrey, I don't think I can bear it."

"You must, dearest. We can't very well leave you here on the road," said Audrey. "Here, let me help you."

With the pale Emmeline stretched out on the forward-facing seat, Audrey called, "Take it slowly, Cal."

"Don't listen to her, Cal; let's get this trip over with as quickly as possible," Emmeline moaned, covering her face with a damp cloth. "I wouldn't feel like this if I were up on the box," she added, her voice more pitiful than ever.

The carriage lurched forward, and they continued on their slow journey.

Audrey said briskly, "I shall read to you, Emmeline. That will take your mind off the motion of the carriage."

"Nothing will take my mind off that . . . unless they will let me take the ribbons."

"No!" chorused all listeners.

Emmeline sighed loudly and replaced the damp cloth.

"An excellent idea, Audrey," said Riggs, the mousy woman who had suffered through years as Emmeline's governess and now acted as her companion.

Seated beside Audrey in the rear-facing seat, the older woman listened avidly as Audrey began to read Miss Austen's *Pride and Prejudice.* Emmeline seemed to benefit from the diversion, too, and soon removed the damp kerchief, her eyes still closed, but a smile curving her lips from time to time as Audrey read aloud about the strong-willed heroine, Elizabeth Bennet.

The carriage was rolling past numerous buildings before Emmeline raised up on the seat, exclaiming in delight that their trip was almost over.

"Would you care to make a small wager about the number of invitations already waiting for us?" she asked.

"I daresay there will be a few since your parents are already in London. Your mother will have spread the word that we are arriving," said Riggs, patting her gray hair into place primly.

"All I want is a hot bath and a soft bed," said Audrey, closing the book and stretching.

"Not for me!" said Emmeline. "A nice gallop around the park would set me to rights!"

"Emmeline!" exclaimed the outraged Riggs. "You mustn't!"

"Why not? If I were a boy—"

"But you are not! Please, Audrey, you must prevail upon her—"

"Do not exert yourself, Riggs. Emmeline is only teasing you. She knows very well that while she may rage about the disparity between her actions and those of her brothers, she will do nothing to put herself beyond the pale."

Emmeline grinned sheepishly while Riggs pursed her lips and turned her head to gaze out the window.

"I'm sorry, Riggs, I shan't tease you anymore. I know you have no sense of humor," said Emmeline, her eyes twinkling.

Riggs turned eagle eyes on her charge and said stiffly, "Emmeline, I do not appreciate your levity. I have a very nice sense of humor, but it does not run to mocking my elders."

"Well, there you have it," said Emmeline, leaning forward and patting her companion's clasped hands. "I don't think of you as my 'elder,' simply as my friend. And I do apologize."

Audrey watched in amusement as Riggs's face melted into a smile. It had always been thus. Riggs was some far-removed relation to the family, too distant to be named, only recognized. In need of employ, she had first come to work as Emmeline's governess. Then, when Emmeline had gone away to school, Riggs had remained as companion to her aunt Patricia, helping "even the numbers," in their overwhelmingly masculine household, as her uncle Gilbert called it.

Riggs was a good influence on Emmeline, her sagacious presence helping to curb the headstrong young woman who always wanted to follow in her brothers' footsteps, even when they led somewhere totally unacceptable for a female.

Audrey thought she understood Riggs, and Emmeline, too. Audrey was often held up to Emmeline as a paragon, a role she took pains to cast off; she much preferred being Emmeline's cousin and friend. It was much more amusing; with Emmeline around, things were never dull. And if she sometimes dragged Audrey into some scrape, it was never intentional.

The carriage stopped in front of a fashionable town house in Grosvenor Square. The footman just managed to let down the steps before his mistress hopped to the ground.

"Beamish! It has been far too long!" exclaimed Emmeline as she rushed up the front steps and into the elegant town house. The butler put out his hand to fend off a possible embrace; Emmeline caught it and pumped it heartily before sailing past to greet her mother who was shaking her head wearily.

"My dear child! What are we to do with her, Beamish?" said the stout matron as she embraced her only daughter. "Just let me look at you! You have been on some slimming regimen, I'll be bound!"

"Just a little; it was the wretched journey which did the rest. Cal refused to let me drive, so . . ."

Her mother only shook her head, and said, "But what have you done with Audrey and Riggs?"

"They are much too slow," said Emmeline, turning to watch their more stately entrance.

"Welcome to London, Audrey. I trust your journey was comfortable."

"It was fine, Aunt Patricia; only a delay or two," said Audrey, glancing at Emmeline as she spoke.

"Are you all right now, Emmeline?" asked her mother, her hand going to the girl's forehead.

"I am fine, just fine. I don't know why everyone will make such a fuss. We muddled along quite well, didn't we, Riggs?"

Riggs smiled benignly on the girl, all thought of their recent contretemps clearly forgotten. "I do believe Emmeline is getting better about traveling."

"You mean she did not spend the entire journey wheedling everyone about sitting up on the box and driving?" This was greeted by a guilty silence, and Patricia Kelsey laughed. "Come along. You'll be wanting to rest after such an arduous trip. I have put you in the rose chamber, Audrey. Eileen, you are in the blue."

"It is still ages till dinner, Mama; can't we go to the shops?"

"No, not today. Tomorrow morning will be soon enough, miss Impatience. We have a few guests coming for dinner."

"Who?" asked Emmeline.

"No one of interest to you, miss. Unless you have a penchant for elderly gentlemen. I understand the admiral's wife is feeling poorly," teased her mother.

Audrey listened with appreciation to this repartee. She had often wished for such a conversation with her own mother. But her mother had ever been serious, never bantering. Audrey and her father had often kidded each other, but his jesting tended to turn mocking, making her uncomfortable.

Still, she thought, lying down on the feather bed after enjoying the luxury of a full bath, she was here now, in London, with her favorite relatives. Only her own amusement need concern her now. That, and choosing a husband.

"Damn!" said Charles quietly, letting the letter fall onto the table.

"What is it? Your dear grandmother coming for a nice, long visit?" asked William hopefully.

"No, not her. It's the other one," said Charles.

"Other one?" asked his friend, spearing another serving of beef before looking up again.

"I told you about her, the one I'm supposed to be betrothed to."

William sputtered and choked, slapping at his shoulders ineffectually until the footman came forward and delivered a resounding blow. Greedily sucking in air, William said weakly, "I thought you were only joking. You know, battlefield regrets and such."

Charles dismissed the footman, wishing he had thought to do so before mentioning the old betrothal. When they were alone, he said, "Joking? I would have had to be a dashed sight closer to death to joke about such a matter."

He ran his fingers through his blond hair and shook his head. "It's not that I really care, you know. I mean, a fellow has to set up his nursery some time or other. It's just that right now is not that 'other' time. I'm much too busy to worry about a fiancée."

"Then don't agree to it. After all, she can't really

be expecting an offer. You've been home over a year and done nothing about it up to now."

"True, only look at this," said Charles, handing over the letter from Rupert Langston.

William perused the boldly written note. Then he shook his head. "He's not exactly calling in his markers," he said.

"No? Then how do you interpret this? 'I expect you will want to call on Audrey; she will be staying with her uncle, Gilbert Kelsey in Grosvenor Square.' "

"Perhaps he means just a social call," said William optimistically.

Charles favored him with a look of derision. "No father writes to a single gentleman asking him to 'call' on his very proper daughter unless he assumes there is some permanent arrangement between them."

"You may have something there," said Will, leaning back in his chair, his hands clasped behind his neck. " 'Course, that's the way of the world. I mean, it stands to reason; here is plain *Mister* Langston with a daughter as good as wed to a title. Stands to reason he would call in the marker sooner or later. I'm surprised your starchy grandmother countenanced a match with a commoner."

"The Langston family could have had a title any number of times. They turned it down, said it couldn't possibly add to their consequence, or so the story goes."

"Whew! And you're to wed a member of this presumptuous family. I'm surprised they would accept you," said William, his tone laced with sarcasm.

"Will, your quick mind astonishes me at times."

"No need to get testy, Charles, just because you've got a case of bridegroom's nerves."

"Shaddup!"

"My, my," murmured Sir William. "Have you ever seen the chit?"

"The last time I saw Audrey Langston, she was ten or eleven years old. I was sent down from school, you remember. I tried to hide out at Drake's tomb, but my grandmother discovered my whereabouts and hauled me home."

"I remember the incident, but I was too busy dealing with my own parents' spleen to worry about you."

"Ah, well, we survived," said Charles, laughing.

"So here she is, on your doorstep, so to speak."

"And just when things are going so famously with the restaurant, now I have to deal with this awkward situation," complained the earl.

"You know, Charles, you may as well look the girl over. I mean, seems to be tied up so neatly. Could be she'll be just the one you've been looking for."

"That's just it, you nodcock, I haven't been looking at all." Charles stood up and paced the length of the room. Finally, he paused, gazing out the French doors leading to the small garden. "You know, it might not be such a bad thing. I have been thinking lately of settling down," he said, not confessing that it was thanks to the sensual Colette his thoughts had been turning in that direction.

But he was an earl; he really couldn't consider Colette for a wife. And if Miss Langston had been trained to be a proper English wife, he might be able to both have his cake and eat it, too. Other men had their mistresses, and their wives turned a blind eye.

Still staring out the window, Charles said, "I shall have to pay Miss Langston a call. It's the least I can do in the circumstances."

"One week, Emmeline, and he has yet to call. I must assume he doesn't wish to acknowledge the connection," said Audrey, looking past her cousin to her aunt and Riggs on the other side of the drawing room. She took another stitch on the sampler she was working on.

Frowning, Emmeline looked at the tiny stitches and commented, "Did you mean for the moon to be black?"

"What? No, of course not. I wasn't paying attention," said Audrey, pulling the thread out of the needle and picking at the stitches. She held it up to the light, brushing away the remaining fibers.

Emmeline chuckled. "It sounds to me as if you are disappointed, Aude. I thought that was what you wanted, to be free to make your own choice."

"True, but it has been very . . . convenient, always knowing there was Lord Middlehurst waiting in the wings. Now I must exert a little more effort to attract someone. And then there is the matter of my diminutive dowry," said Audrey.

Emmeline laughed, the sound hearty rather than

delicate, bringing their quiet conversation to Riggs's attention.

"Emmeline, you are not in the stables now. Please be so good as to remember that a young lady's amusement is shown quietly."

"Yes, Riggs," said Emmeline demurely. Grinning at Audrey, she leaned closer and whispered, "Now, none of that. We'll find someone who won't care a fig about your fortune. He will fall madly in love with you, for your beauty and wit alone."

Audrey couldn't help smiling at the determination in her cousin's voice, but she said sensibly, "Is this your first Season? You must have forgotten; beauty and wit are not the usual foundation for marriage in our circles."

"Just wait. Tomorrow night is Wednesday. We'll begin our hunt at Almack's. Anyone who might possibly be worthy of us will be in attendance. Just think, Aude, tomorrow night we may meet our future husbands!"

Unable to ignore Emmeline's contagious enthusiasm, Audrey found herself drawn into a conversation about their dream husbands.

Later, however, in the quiet of her bedchamber, the old doubts assailed her. She certainly couldn't count on Middlehurst. And who else might be willing to overlook the fact that she had no fortune to accompany the estate she would someday inherit? She would have to look about her for someone with a fortune of his own. And exactly how did one find out that the man one had just shared a country dance with was possessed of a tidy sum?

She tossed and turned on this problem. By morning, she would gladly have throttled Middlehurst for callously ignoring their arrangement and thus forcing her into this uncomfortable situation. Dragging herself to the breakfast table, she groaned her request for coffee and toast.

"There's a letter for you in the morning's post, my dear," said her uncle Gilbert.

"For me? Is it from Mama?"

"I don't think so. I believe it was sent from somewhere in London. You'll just have to open it to see."

Audrey frowned at the unfamiliar seal before tearing into the envelope. Sleep fled as she read:

Dear Miss Langston,

I look forward to renewing our acquaintance now that you have come to London.

Your Servant,
Middlehurst

"Who is it from, my dear, if you don't mind my asking?" said her uncle.

Audrey handed him the note; he nodded in approval.

"What can it mean?" she asked, her eyes wide with confusion. She thought she had come to terms with the fact that Middlehurst would not call, that he had no interest in pursuing their agreement.

"I would say the gentleman has done what is proper. He wouldn't want to mention the arrangement; that would be too forward. This way, you will have a chance to become acquainted with him first."

Her uncle watched her in silence for a moment before adding. "I haven't met Middlehurst, but I understand he has a good reputation. There were a few stories . . ."

"Stories?" asked Audrey.

"Oh, just the usual pranks. I'm sure he's grown up since then."

"Pranks? Oh, Uncle Gilly, I don't know about this. He doesn't sound like the kind of man I could—"

"All you need do is meet him. If you can't like him, I'm certain your father will sort things out. And you know you may count on me," he said, rising and passing behind her on his way to the door; he gave her shoulder a gentle squeeze. "Just give the man a chance."

"I will," she said tremulously. "Thank you, Uncle."

"Rimbeau, what do you mean, we can't serve tonight?"

"No, no, I said we couldn't serve the usual menu, sir. Colette went to every vendor, but no one had the fish we planned to serve."

"Then what did she buy?"

"The beef, that is no problem; or the fowl. It is just the fish."

"So what do we have? Something we haven't served before?" demanded Charles.

"Exactly, sir. Oysters. That was all they had that was fresh enough."

"Colette!" barked Charles, sounding every inch

the earl and not caring when the other workers jumped in surprise.

"Yes, sir?" said the dark beauty, her nostrils flaring slightly to show her displeasure.

"What the deuce do you mean, coming back without the haddock or something similar? I thought you could wrangle a bargain with the devil himself!"

"And so I can, Mr. Brown," she said slowly, lingering over his name as if she knew him to be an impostor. "But I cannot conjure up haddock when there is none. I don't know why there was no fish up to our standards; there simply wasn't any to be had. Unless, of course, you wished to serve less than the very best tonight!"

Charles's glare faded, and his dark blue eyes sparkled with appreciation. "Touché," he said quietly. Then, rubbing his hands together, he said matter-of-factly, "Very well, then oysters we shall serve. Now, Rimbeau, just how the deuce do you suggest we prepare these slippery little fellows?"

"I know a sauce, sir, that will have the diners clamoring for more!" said Rimbeau, kissing his fingertips loudly.

"Then let's get busy!"

Charles rolled up his sleeves and tied on his apron. He looked over his shoulder and grinned at Colette who was watching his every move. Unabashed, she tilted her head and continued her scrutiny. Charles looked around from time to time, catching her eyes fixed on him as he worked.

Evening fell, and still Charles remained, reluctant to leave the easy camaraderie of the kitchen, his kitchen. Colette, dressed now in a soft yellow gown to greet their customers, floated into the kitchen every few minutes, favoring him with a knowing smile.

"You should be going, sir," she said on one of her forays into the kitchen.

"In just a few minutes," said Charles.

"There is a Lady Fenton who insists she will discover the identity of our marvelous chef. I am afraid she may come back . . ."

"Oh, very well," he said, wiping his hands.

He paused as Colette untied his apron, her hands brushing his back as she reached around him to place it on the counter.

"Thank you," said Charles, turning. The heady scent of her light perfume mingled with the spices; she read his mind and smiled.

"Any time I may be of service to you, Mr. Brown," she said, slipping away and disappearing into the dining rooms.

Charles took a deep breath, waved a silent good-bye to Rimbeau, and hurried out the back door. Handie was there with the cab, walking the horse up and down.

"Yer late t'night, Mr. Brown."

"Oh? What time is it?"

"Nigh on ten o'clock."

"The devil you say! Home, and quickly, Handie!"

"I told you I didn't expect him to be here," said Audrey, sipping the tasteless orgeat which Almack's served for the ladies' refreshment.

"It is not yet eleven o'clock, Audrey. He is probably just running late."

"I'm sure I couldn't care in the least. It is not as if he owes me the courtesy of being here. After all, he didn't say he would see me at Almack's. He didn't even say when he might call," said Audrey, putting on her best smile for the short, round Lord Leffington, who had persistently pursued her all evening. She set aside her glass and smoothed her demure blue silk evening gown that matched her eyes perfectly.

She glanced at Emmeline who was all smiles, her amusement at Audrey's predicament all too evident. Never mind, thought Audrey, that Lord Leffington is a dreadful bore or that we look preposterous on the dance floor together, I being such a long Meg and he being so stout. At least Lord Leffington has done me the courtesy of showing up and asking me to dance!

Emmeline took a long sip of her drink to hide her smile. Then she set it down to greet Mr. Grant, a gentleman almost as horse-mad as she was. It didn't hurt that he was quite handsome, too.

The four stood up for the quadrille, a dance which lasted until the servants were set to close the doors to Almack's. After eleven o'clock, no one, not even Wellington himself, could gain admittance into the hallowed halls.

Just as the servants moved to close the heavy doors, Audrey looked across the ballroom. In walked one of the most handsome men she had ever seen; her hand slipped off Lord Leffington's crooked arm.

"Miss Langston, Miss Langston," said the round Lord Leffington.

It seemed the candlelight shone through his eyes. Muscles rippled beneath the cloth of his knee breeches and stockings. His black coat strained against broad shoulders.

"What?" she responded, clearly in another world. She stepped away from Leffington, moving toward the doors.

"Audrey!" whispered Emmeline, hooking arms with her cousin and turning her neatly. "Whatever are you thinking?"

Audrey regained her senses, blinking once or twice before responding. "I don't know, really. I saw—"

"Well, get hold of yourself! You don't want to start people talking!" said Emmeline, her husky voice causing people's heads to turn.

"Of course not. Thank you, Emmeline." Audrey moved away to stand beside her aunt, her eyes flicking over the assembly, searching for the man who had taken her breath away. There was something familiar about him; she felt she knew him. Then he was there, by her side.

"Miss Langston, I daresay you don't remember me," Charles began, bowing from the waist before placing a kiss on the back of her hand.

"Middlehurst," she said flatly. How could she not have recognized him? He had changed, to be sure, but there was still that golden blond hair and those bright, blue eyes.

"Yes, it is I. I dem . . . er . . . almost didn't manage

to get inside; two minutes later, and they would have barred the door on me."

"Oh, well, that's good then." I am talking like an idiot, thought Audrey, wondering why her wits had suddenly gone to let He wasn't a god, for goodness' sake!

"Have you been in London long?" he asked.

"A week, perhaps. I am staying with my aunt and uncle."

"Yes, I know," said Charles, wondering if the affliction of being tongue-tied was catching.

"And how long have you been back in England?" asked Audrey, congratulating herself on coming back to her senses.

"A little over a year. I stayed in Paris for some months after Napoleon's surrender."

"Have you visited Drake's Park?" she asked, knowing full well that if he had so much as set foot in the tiny village of Twickham, she would have heard of it.

"No, that is not my favorite place, I'm afraid. It's so dreadfully dreary 'round there," he added. "Oh, sorry, I forgot about your home being so close and all. I'm sure your estate is anything but dreary."

An awkward silence fell between them. Then the orchestra struck up a waltz, and Audrey accepted his invitation to dance.

"You waltz very well," said Charles after they had completed one revolution of the dance floor.

"Thank you. So do you."

He nodded, his eyes twinkling.

"What is it?" she asked as he continued to smile

down at her. It was odd, and refreshing, to waltz with a man taller than she was.

"I was just thinking how awkward all this is. I mean, you know why I am here; I know why you are here. Perhaps if we just admit we are sizing each other up, we can manage to actually enjoy our waltz," said Charles.

Audrey's polite smile widened; they dropped their masks and began to relax.

"Much better," said Charles, tightening his hold on her slightly. "I find it much easier to lay one's cards on the table, so to speak."

"It is rather exhilarating," said Audrey, laughing. "I have been dreading meeting you." At his quizzical look, she added hastily, "That is, I was apprehensive about it. My father merely told me he wrote to you; he didn't tell me what he had said."

"And you would very much like to know what was in that letter," said Charles, executing a complicated turn which she followed easily.

Breathless and laughing, Audrey admitted, "Well, yes, but I suppose it is terribly forward of me to even mention it."

"Not at all, Miss Langston, since it does concern your future."

The music stopped, and they began the obligatory promenade. Charles remained silent until they had almost reached her aunt.

"I shall ask your aunt if I may take you for a drive tomorrow morning, shall I?"

"That would be nice," Audrey said formally, wishing they were still dancing and chatting amiably.

He bowed before her aunt, making a few polite comments before asking permission to call and take Audrey driving. Their plans sealed, he bowed again and walked away, speaking to an acquaintance or two. Soon afterward, Audrey saw him leave.

Obviously, he had come to Almack's for one purpose—to meet her. She felt an odd warmth spring to life in her breast. She glanced around to see if anyone was watching her, then unfurled her fan and applied it lazily. The feeling passed.

To attend Almack's, single out one young lady, and then depart was tantamount to a declaration as far as the rest of the Ton was concerned. Had others noticed? Judging from the speculative stares she intercepted, they had.

By the time news of their drive on the morrow spread, she and the Earl of Middlehurst would be the talk of every club and drawing room in London!

"Tell me everything!" exclaimed Emmeline, slipping into Audrey's room and rushing to join her on the bed.

"Please, I am too tired to talk. I need to go to sleep," protested Audrey.

"Rubbish!" Emmeline dragged part of the counterpane across her legs, propping herself up on one elbow, ready to receive Audrey's news.

Audrey, who was anything but ready for sleep, stared at her cousin in silence. How could she explain her impressions and feelings to Emmeline when she didn't understand them herself?

But there was no denying her cousin, so she began, "What do you want to know?"

"What was it like, dancing in his arms? He is ever so handsome; I vow, Audrey, if you were not betrothed to the man, I would try to attract him myself!"

"My, he did make an impression on you," said Audrey, playing for time.

"What did he say? Should I wish you happy?"

"Good heavens, no! We only danced!"

"But it was the waltz; surely you conversed," said Emmeline, her voice tinged with disappointment.

"Of course. I asked him when he had returned from the continent. He asked how long I had been in London."

Emmeline sat up straight and swung her legs over the side of the bed as she said, "How utterly tedious of you, Audrey! I think you and the dull earl will make a matched pair." She flounced to the door.

A matched pair, mused Audrey, her heart's beats doing a jig at the thought. Dull? Tedious? Oh, no, not if the earl could feel for her what she already was feeling for him!

Four

Thursday morning brought rain, and Audrey was not surprised when a messenger arrived with a note from Middlehurst postponing their drive. After all, they could not go for one in a closed carriage; that would have been a social solecism.

Audrey had to be satisfied with his promise to call if the ladies were having an "at home" in the afternoon. She took special care with her toilette, taking down her hair three times before she was satisfied with the outcome.

Lunch was served in the morning room. Uncle Gil had returned to Blackthorn to tend to some problem with the planting. Aunt Patricia was lunching in her rooms. Audrey and Emmeline, therefore, were reduced to their own company.

"You are very quiet today," said Emmeline finally.

"So are you," returned Audrey. "It is just the rain, I suppose."

"And the fact that you cannot go for your drive with the resplendent Lord Middlehurst," teased Emmeline.

"I am not so enamored as that after a single waltz!" said Audrey sharply.

"Ah, but you admit to being enamored to some degree," Emmeline retorted.

Audrey tried to frown down her cousin, but she ruined her act, breaking into a grin. "You are a sore trial to me," she said.

"Well, at least one of us should be having some success in our quest," Emmeline declared.

"But what about that handsome, horse-lover, Mr. Grant?" teased Audrey. "I noticed that he asked you to dance twice last night."

"True, but the second time, he began speaking of his home in Leicester and of how very expensive it is to keep all his hunters, to secure the best breeding stock, and so forth."

"Well, I assume that is true," said Audrey sensibly.

"Yes, of course it is, but he knows I am aware of all that," said Emmeline, striving to sound detached, but not fooling herself or Audrey. "He was only preparing me for the inevitable. He may enjoy my company, but when it comes to choosing a wife, he must find one with enough of the ready to add to his stables!"

"Emmeline! Such language," said Riggs, entering silently. "You really must try to curb this tendency to use cant. I know your brothers flavor their speech . . . Well, really!" added Riggs as Emmeline fled the room.

"Forgive her, Riggs. She has been rebuffed by her Mr. Grant. She's not herself at the moment."

"Poor child. I'll go to her," said the spinster, rising.

"I should think she would prefer a bit of privacy

first," said Audrey. "You know she hates to display her feminine emotions."

"True, true. Emmeline is unique in that respect. I have often told her she must remember that a few tears, well placed, can take a young woman far."

"I know, I know. But you must admire her spirit."

The older woman's face softened. "Admire her? I think Emmeline is one of the finest young ladies I know. She is honest and courageous, not to mention beautiful!" Dabbing at her eyes with a scrap of lace, Riggs hurried out of the room, leaving Audrey to her own thoughts.

As she had often remarked in the past, "enjoying the Season" was a misnomer. There were too many hopes dashed, too many hearts broken.

It was not that Emmeline was in love with Mr. Grant; she had shown no sign of love, but she enjoyed his company. And he had effectively delivered the message that he must hang out for a rich wife, that he would no longer be courting, however casually, Emmeline. And once he had chosen his bride, he and Emmeline could no longer be friends.

"Audrey, we should gather in the salon. Our callers will begin arriving soon," said Aunt Patricia.

Audrey rose and joined her aunt. Emmeline, her face freshly washed, was also present. Riggs sat by the fire, her mending in her hand. She was not required to do the family mending, but she declared that it made her feel useful, and so she took care of it all.

"You look very nice in that yellow gown, Audrey. I loved to wear that pale yellow when I was a girl," said Aunt Patricia.

"You could still wear it," said Audrey.

"No, not at my age. Certain colors are for the young girls, others for matrons, and never the twain shall meet."

"Except at a masquerade," said Emmeline, her dark eyes twinkling. "I think we should host a masquerade, Mama. It would be the perfect entertainment for us, since neither Audrey nor I are in our first Seasons."

"A masquerade is too fast," said Riggs, looking up sharply.

"Not if one does it correctly," said Emmeline. "What do you think, Aude? Couldn't we have a proper masquerade ball?"

"I'm not certain what you mean by proper," said Audrey cautiously.

"I think I know exactly what she means," laughed Aunt Patricia. "But I don't think it would be very wise. We might have a ball, perhaps, to celebrate some special occasion."

Audrey and Emmeline exchanged grimaces, neither one at all willing to speculate that there might be a "special occasion" looming in her near future.

The door opened, and Beamish intoned regally, "Lady Anne Hampton and the Misses Hampton, madam."

"Anne, how good of you to call," said Aunt Patricia, and the games began.

For the next two hours, Audrey smiled, murmured, and nodded, a pattern card of elegant behavior for an unmarried lady. Emmeline, forgetting momentarily the defection of Mr. Grant, was a little too loud, a little too boisterous, and the center of a lively group of young ladies and gentlemen.

Guests conveniently ignored the polite rule of remaining only thirty minutes; Aunt Patricia's "at homes" were legendary. No one wanted to miss the excellent refreshments which seemed to never dwindle; and the company, though not the top of the trees, was lively and animated. Everyone went away feeling full and content.

Audrey, on the other hand, watched them depart with a mixture of relief and pain. It was difficult keeping her polite mask in place when her heart did a somersault each time Beamish opened the parlor door to announce another arrival.

"I don't know when I have been more entertained, Mama!" exclaimed Emmeline, favoring her mother with a quick kiss on the cheek. "Everyone says you are the very best of hostesses! Don't they, Audrey?"

"Thank you, dear," said Aunt Patricia, intercepting Emmeline's attention. "Audrey, dear, you are a bit pale. You aren't catching a chill, are you?"

"No, Aunt, I am fine. A little tired, perhaps."

"Why don't you lie down until dinner?"

"Yes, I think I shall."

"But, Mama, I wanted to go to the shops and look for a new bonnet."

"There is no reason you and I can't do so," said her mother, shooing Emmeline out the door. "Run change your gown, and we will go. Audrey, do you need anything?"

"No, thank you, Aunt," said Audrey following Emmeline up the stairs more leisurely.

"I'll keep an eye on her, Patricia," said Riggs, emerging from the salon.

"Thank you, Eileen. You know, I am usually very mild tempered, but Middlehurst is one young man I would gladly throttle right now!"

Middlehurst stretched and removed the soiled apron. He sat down at his desk, glad he had replaced the uncomfortable chair with one much larger and more padded. Pulling the ledger books forward, he checked the figures, making notes in the margin here and there.

The columns were perfectly aligned and correctly totaled. Each time he bent closer to the bound paper, he caught the scent, ever so faint, of Colette's perfume.

Finished, he sat back, closing his eyes.

"Is everything to your satisfaction, Mr. Brown?"

Charles sat bolt upright in the chair, blinking his eyes. "You startled me, Colette. You should make some noise when you enter a room, warn a fellow."

"I did knock quietly, but you did not answer, sir."

"I suppose I nodded off," he said, rising and indicating the chair next to the old, battered desk. "I just have a few questions."

Colette pulled the chair closer, leaning forward until their shoulders almost touched. Charles inhaled her fragrance, a light, flowery scent.

"Now that, my . . . Mr. Brown, that was money expended for the new linens. You remember we added several tables to the main dining room when we moved the long table to the private dining room."

"Yes, of course. I didn't think we could have worn out any cloths that quickly." He turned a page, and Colette moved closer, her knee touching his, her perfume invading his senses.

"That mark indicates a loss," she said, her voice so businesslike, Charles forgot his distraction. "I purchased half-a-dozen fine geese, and only four were prepared. Unfortunately, that sometimes happens. This entry also, only it was the lamb."

"Is there anything we can do to prevent such losses?" asked Charles, sitting back and studying her.

"Short of keeping our own livestock, no. But you see here? These last entries reflect how well we did the first month. To make such a profit, my . . . Mr. Brown, in such a short time, is very unusual."

"Much of it is due to your efforts, Colette." When she blinded him with a dazzling smile, he added hastily, "And your father's, of course."

"Of course," she said, her pleasure tempered. "Is there anything else?" she asked, rising.

"No, that's all. You keep excellent records."

"Thank you. Then I will bid you good evening, sir."

"Evening? What time is it?"

"Almost six o'clock."

"Blast!" exclaimed Charles, jumping to his feet. Then his shoulders sagged, and he slumped back into his chair again, frowning.

"Did you miss an appointment, sir?" asked Colette.

Charles looked up sharply as if surprised to find her still in his office.

"What? No. That is, I had promised to pay a call on someone." He sighed. "Too late now."

"I am sorry, sir. If you had told me, I could have reminded you."

Charles stood up hurriedly, picked up his hat and coat, and headed for the door, muttering, "No, dash it all, shouldn't have to be reminded. Good night, Colette."

"Good night, Mr. Brown," she murmured, watching him until the back door closed.

Entering the office, Colette strolled to the desk and sat down behind it. Leaning forward and resting her chin on her clasped hands, she said softly, "So, there is another woman in your life, Lord Middlehurst. I wonder what she is like. Probably one of those very proper, very English misses."

Colette sat up straight and her dark eyes narrowed as if she could see the earl's new woman. Then a slow smile spread across her face. She was aware of the effect she had on the earl.

"Perhaps being a countess would be a very pleasant pastime."

Audrey blew out the candles and climbed into bed. The rain made everything cold and damp, and she shivered, pulling the covers up to her chin and closing her eyes.

Moments later she opened them, threw back the counterpane, and fumbled for the tinderbox to relight the candles. Then she picked up the novel beside her bed and began to read. Fifteen minutes later—she had timed herself by the chiming clock on the mantel—she let the book slip from her fingers.

Rising, she moved to the dressing table and released the heavy, silvery braid. Picking up the brush, she began counting the strokes.

Then, stopping in midstroke, she made a moue at her image and said sternly, "It is no use. You are such a ninny to fall in love with a man after a twenty-minute acquaintance. I never thought you could be such a ninnyhammer!" She counted four more strokes and replaced the brush on the table.

"And now you are talking to yourself!" she said, but she made a face in the mirror and smiled.

There was a swift knock, and the door burst open, propelling Emmeline into the room.

"You should have gone!" she declared, waltzing across the floor and flopping down inelegantly on the mussed bed.

From her vantage point, Audrey laughed at the flash of stockinged legs and petticoat.

"If I missed that show, I must have missed the rout of the Season!" she teased.

"Not at all," said Emmeline, sitting up and pulling her gown into place. *"He* was there!"

"Who?" asked Audrey, unconcerned.

"Middlehurst!" announced Emmeline grandly.

"Oh," Audrey replied with feigned disinterest, "I thought you were speaking of Mr. Grant."

"Heavens, no! I haven't thought of him in ages. I meant Middlehurst. You will never guess what he said."

"I'm sure I would not waste time inquiring about

Lord Middlehurst's conversation," said Audrey, her tone haughty.

"Oh, very well," said Emmeline, climbing off the bed. "Then I will bid you good night."

Gritting her teeth, Audrey watched as her cousin drifted casually toward the door. Emmeline turned the handle and paused, clearly torn between maintaining her dignity and her need to divest herself of some great news.

"Are you certain you don't wish to know what he told my mother?" she asked, cocking her head to one side, her dark eyes hopeful.

Audrey relented. "Oh, very well." It would be churlish not to listen, she told herself.

Emmeline hurried toward the dressing table, pulling forward a straight-backed chair.

"Middlehurst asked Mama where you were," she breathed out.

"He did?"

"Yes, and when Mama told him you were indisposed, he said he was so sorry, for he very much wanted to see you this evening since he had been obliged to miss our 'at home,' " said Emmeline, sitting back with a sigh of satisfaction.

"But why was he obliged to miss it?" said the skeptic.

"Oh, Aude, do not be a prude! He was probably gambling away a fortune at his club or shooting at Manton's Gallery, or some such. You know what gentlemen are."

"Nevertheless, he found something else more enjoyable than calling on me—I mean, us. I think I shall reserve judgment about Middlehurst until I have become better acquainted with him," she said loftily.

"Well, that will not take long," said Emmeline, smiling like the cat that swallowed the cream.

"Why?" said Audrey with narrowed eyes.

"Mama gave her permission for us to make up part of a party for Vauxhall next week. On Tuesday, I think."

"Well, there is nothing singular about Middlehurst issuing such an invitation. I'm sure there will be any number of young ladies present."

Emmeline's smile widened. "I don't think so. He mentioned only his friend, Sir William Compton—oh, you must see him; he is divine!—and another gentleman and his sister."

"Probably the intended of Sir William," said Audrey, who had had quite enough of Emmeline lording it over her with her news.

Emmeline looked crushed, then tried for a disdainful expression, and said, "I couldn't care less what Sir William's status is." She looked down, frowning.

Audrey patted her cousin's hand, saying, "I doubt that Sir William is betrothed. We haven't read any announcements in the paper at all. What does he look like?"

Emmeline happily rattled off all of Sir William's physical attributes and then began to catalogue the list of his supposed virtues.

Lending only half an ear, Audrey let her prattle on. Her first instinct told her to refuse to go to Vauxhall. Such a childish reaction puzzled her; she was not usually vindictive. And after all, what allegiance did he owe her? He had not promised to call. She wondered momentarily exactly how he had passed the rainy afternoon. She was not supposed to know about such things, but she could not escape the suspicion that he may have been with a mistress.

"You haven't heard a word I have said," said Emmeline, tapping Audrey's knee.

"Oh, I'm sorry, Em. I was wool-gathering."

"And I know about whom," teased Emmeline.

Audrey rose and crossed the room to the window. Pulling the curtains aside, she stared into the rain-soaked garden.

"I'm not accustomed to feeling . . . I can't even identify it."

"Love?" asked Emmeline.

"Ah, you sound amazed. And so am I, Emmeline. Who would have thought such feelings could happen so quickly. I never believed in love at first sight. A *coup de foudre,* the French call it; a clap of thunder." Her eyes filling with tears, Audrey turned and faced her cousin. "A very appropriate description, don't you think?"

Emmeline hurried to Audrey's side, putting an arm around her slender waist.

Looking down, Audrey said helplessly, "I feel so foolish."

"You? Never! If you have fallen in love with Middlehurst, then we must give him every opportunity to do the same! How can he help but love you, Aude? Just wait and see; Middlehurst will be eating out of your hand in no time!"

"I would settle for a return of my regard," said

Audrey, brushing away her tears and the megrims with a smile.

"I don't know how I shall be able to manage everything, William," said Charles, putting the finishing touches on his cravat. "I meant to call on Miss Langston before tonight, but the restaurant. . . . For all I know, she may have taken me in dislike after my being so inattentive."

Sir William looked up from the game of patience he had set out on the earl's escritoire. "Perhaps you should give up the restaurant; Rimbeau can run it for you."

Charles turned away from the mirror and glared at his friend. "I can't do that! I won't! What do you think has kept me sane these last few months? No, I can't give it up. She'll just have to understand."

"So you're going to tell the elegant Miss Langston that you are a chef?"

"Deuce take you, Will! You know I can't do that! I'll just have to . . . Oh, devil take it!" exclaimed the earl, ripping the ruined cravat from his neck.

"Well, whatever else happens, you had better bestir yourself, or we'll be late taking them up for tonight's adventure!"

"What was I thinking, Emmeline? This color is absolutely frightful!"

"It is exquisite, Audrey. And you look wonderful!"

"But the neckline, it is so . . . modest," she said,

looking at her image and tugging at the offending garment.

"It is charming," said Emmeline, standing behind her cousin and studying her own image with a frown. "Do you like my hair? When Jane Simmons wore hers this way, I thought it was so very elegant. Now, I'm not certain. What do you think?"

"It's very nice," said Audrey, barely sparing a glance at Emmeline's dark curls.

"You don't think it makes me look lopsided?"

Audrey sighed volubly and turned, smoothing the rose overskirt of her gown, a soft rose which set off her fair complexion and silvery blond hair to perfection.

"We both look magnificent," she declared, seizing Emmeline by the shoulders and propelling her gently away from the mirror.

Emmeline grinned. "We were acting rather silly, weren't we?"

Their young abigail peered into the chamber with an exclamation of admiration and said, "Miss Emmeline, miss Audrey, the gentlemen have arrived."

"Thank you, Millie," said Emmeline, drawing herself up to her full height and offering her arm to her willowy cousin. "Shall we?" she added with a grin.

Audrey took her arm, and they left the security of Emmeline's chamber for the unknown delights of the evening. Below, Riggs was conversing quietly with Sir William and Middlehurst. Pausing at the first landing, the cousins unknowingly sent shivers of delight through the waiting gentlemen.

Audrey, her breath catching in her throat, had the

eeriest sensation, the feeling that she was looking into her own future. Would this rush of emotions always take her breath away when she beheld this man?

Tonight, he was dressed in black, even to his waist-coat, his snowy cravat highlighting his handsome face. He looked up suddenly, a smile transforming it. Wonder flooded her soul, and she smiled in return. Never had she experienced such an instantaneous bond with a man. Charles started forward, meeting them at the last step with a bow.

"I told you we were the luckiest of fellows, Will," he said over his shoulder.

"The very luckiest," said Sir William, answering their curtseys with an elegant bow. He offered his arm to Emmeline, smiling as he looked down at her from his great height. "You have styled your hair a little differently, miss Kelsey; it, and you, are stunning."

Emmeline blinked, a tiny frown furrowing her brow.

"Fustian, Sir William! I am unaccustomed to such flowery compliments; I do not deal in Spanish coin!"

"Emmeline," whispered Riggs urgently.

Sir William broke the awkward silence that followed with a hearty laugh.

"I do believe, Miss Kelsey, you are an original! And though I fear I may incur your wrath by this, I must add, a very delightful original!"

Everyone laughed, wraps were called for, and they were on their way.

* * *

"We are to meet Lord Asherton and his sister Lady Caroline at the Rotunda. I have reserved a box for us. I am sure you ladies have been to Vauxhall before," said Charles, smiling in turn at each of them.

Riggs nodded, saying, "Yes, my lord, we have been fortunate enough to attend the pleasure garden several times in the past, but one never tires of the beauty of the fireworks display or the waterfall."

"Miss Riggs is a great admirer of fireworks displays," said Emmeline, the light of mischief in her eyes. "I remember she was so enamored of them that she took me and my brothers, when we were children, to a fine display on the occasion of the old king's birthday."

"I'm sure the gentlemen do not care to hear about that," said Riggs, becoming flustered.

"No, Miss Riggs, I assure you we would love to hear the story," said Charles, smiling kindly at the older woman.

"There is really no story, my lord. I took Emmeline and her brothers, all very energetic children."

"I can imagine," said Sir William, winking at Emmeline.

"Pray continue," said Charles.

"Andrew, Emmeline, Christopher, and John disappeared. I was frantic, as you may well imagine. With little Elliot in tow, I searched everywhere. Then I heard Emmeline's screams; she and her brothers were up a tree, their faces so close to the fireworks, I could see every detail. Emmeline was the only one with enough sense to be frightened by the flames shooting past them. I attracted the men's attention, and they pulled them to safety."

Giggling, Emmeline said, "And I could see Riggs's face clearly by the fire coming out of her eyes!"

Riggs raised her brows. "At least I still had eyelashes and eyebrows, which is more than I could say for you and your brothers!"

"We were a sad little quartet," admitted Emmeline. "Not only that, but everyone was mad because they had halted the fireworks while they hauled us away!"

"You *were* a madcap," said Sir William, his green eyes crinkling with amusement.

"But now I am all grown up," said Emmeline.

"How much longer, my lord?" asked Audrey, deciding the topic was becoming a little too personal.

"I believe we have arrived," he announced as the carriage came to a halt.

The door opened, and he hopped down, leaving Sir William to help the ladies out while he received them. They proceeded to the Rotunda, Charles with Riggs and Audrey on his arms, and William trailing with Emmeline. Judging from her giggles, she was well pleased with this arrangement.

They were arriving late; the dancing had already begun. After introducing everyone, Lord Asherton asked Emmeline to dance, and Sir William led out Lady Caroline. Charles proved a solicitous host, ordering champagne and serving Riggs and Audrey himself.

"You must tell us about your years in Spain, my lord," said Riggs.

"There is little to tell, really. Between the battles,

we endured many hardships and much boredom. The battles, of course, I would not deign to describe to ladies."

"I assure you, my lord, when Miss Riggs asks about your life on the Peninsula, she wants to hear all about the battles."

"Audrey," protested Riggs, "his lordship will think me unnatural or bloodthirsty."

"Not at all, madam. If you wish to know . . . ?"

"I am extremely interested in the strategy of war, the manner in which the troops are deployed. It is fascinating to me to realize that, while the numbers are important, it is often the brilliance of one general, one man, which decides the battle."

"I see you are a student of strategy. Have you ever met Lord Wellington?"

"No, but I saw him when the celebrations were held," said Riggs.

Audrey, let her attention wander as she listened to his voice, allowing it to caress her ears without paying attention to the words. She breathed deeply, singling out his cologne from the myriad of other odors assailing her senses. His hair, longer than current fashion dictated, was a deep gold. His eyes, though blue, were bright and sparkling. Perhaps others would not find it so, but Audrey thought he was the most handsome man in the land.

"Miss Langston, I fear we are boring you," said Charles, smiling at her gently.

"Oh, no, my lord, I was enjoying watching the dancers," she prevaricated, hoping he had not noticed how closely she had been studying him. Then she blushed. "I do hope I wasn't being rude," she added.

"Not at all, my dear. I am surprised to find a lady as knowledgeable as Miss Riggs on the subject, but I do not expect others, especially ladies, to possess such interest. I am not that knowledgeable myself; I only followed orders, " he said modestly.

"I doubt that, my lord," said Riggs.

"That was delightful," said Lady Caroline, laughing as she entered the box with Sir William.

"Where is Emmeline?" said Audrey, looking beyond Sir William.

"I believe Andrew mentioned that they were going to see the waterfall," said Lady Caroline.

"Just the two of them?" said Riggs, her glance sending Audrey a message.

Audrey rose. "I believe I, too, would like to see the waterfall."

Sir William waved Charles back to his seat, saying quickly, "I will accompany you, Miss Langston."

When they were away from the Rotunda, Audrey asked urgently, "Is there some reason I should worry about my cousin being alone with Lord Asherton?"

William slowed his pace and chuckled. "Actually, I can think of no reason. I suppose I simply wished to be the one to accompany Miss Kelsey." Looking down at her from his great height, for he was even taller than Charles, he gave her a sheepish grin. "Sounds rather daft, I suppose, since I have only met Miss Kelsey on one other occasion. But there you have it, Miss Langston. You have discovered my secret; I am an incurable romantic."

"I would not have guessed, Sir William. Your reputation . . ." Audrey let this thought dangle helplessly.

He shook his head. "Reputations are strange beings, Miss Langston. For instance, Charles has the reputation of being a little aloof, but that is before one becomes well acquainted with him."

Audrey fought the blush that threatened to steal across her cheeks and nodded. "I try not to prejudge anyone, Sir William."

They continued on their way in a companionable silence. Sir William spied Emmeline and Lord Asherton gazing raptly at the artificial waterfall. Audrey moved forward until she was standing just behind the couple. She looked around for Sir William; he took no notice of her, his expression bemused as he watched Emmeline.

"We decided we would join you," said Audrey.

"Oh, I didn't know you would want to come, Audrey. You have not expressed much interest in the past."

"I find it fascinating," commented Lord Asherton. "I can't figure out how they go about it. Listen, that sounds like real thunder."

"I think that is the first volley of the fireworks display," said Sir William, offering his arm to Emmeline and turning toward the sound. "I believe we can see the best of it from our box." She dimpled up at him, and Audrey accepted Lord Asherton's escort.

They returned to the trio in the private box where a dazzling array of thinly sliced ham, cheeses, and sweets awaited.

Sir William guided Emmeline to a chair, saying

heartily, "Ah, sustenance! You have no idea the quantity of nourishment a large body like mine requires. At first I thought the rumbling of the fireworks was my stomach," he quipped, causing Emmeline to giggle.

"May I serve you, Miss Langston?" said Charles, covering his frown at his friend with a smile for Audrey.

"Yes, please, my lord. This is wonderful. Did you try one of the strawberries, Riggs? I know how you adore them."

"Yes, thank you. His lordship has taken care of me very well," said the older woman, smiling fondly at the earl. "He was telling me about the most delicious dining establishment, Chez . . ."

"Canard," supplied Charles. "Actually, it was Lady Caroline who mentioned it first, but we have dined there, also."

"First rate," agreed Lord Asherton.

"Quite nice," said William, grinning at Charles. "I took my aunt; she's a high stickler, and even she blessed the place."

"Sir William!" said Lady Caroline, rapping him playfully on the arm. "Your aunt is one of the nicest ladies I know."

"To you, perhaps, but Aunt Kathryn feels no compunction about abusing her little nephew."

"Little?" said Emmeline, gazing up at him with mischief in her dark eyes. "That is not a word I would ever use to describe you, Sir William. You were in the light cavalry, weren't you?"

"That's right," he said, a smile playing on his lips.

"Must have been a mountain of a horse to carry you into battle," she said, laughing.

"Emmeline! Pray do not be impertinent!" snapped Riggs.

"No, no, Miss Riggs. Miss Kelsey has the right of it. He was a giant; all of seventeen hands."

"Was?" murmured Emmeline, her eyes filling with sudden tears as her compassion for the animal overwhelmed her.

"Emmeline," said Audrey, squeezing her cousin's hand.

Emmeline looked up, her eyes wide as one pendulous tear threatened to fall.

Sir William took her other hand in his large one; leaning close to her ear, he whispered, "I took him home and put him out to pasture last year. He was much too magnificent for London."

"Truly?" whispered Emmeline.

"Truly," said the giant man. "Now, let's eat!"

Over Emmeline's head, Audrey and Charles exchanged a smile.

As their feast continued, Audrey was surprised at how quiet the earl was. He was content to add only a comment or two as Lord Asherton and Sir William dominated the conversation. The earl's constant attention to Riggs only heightened her opinion of him.

"Miss Langston, may I have this dance," he asked when her plate was empty.

"Certainly, my lord," said Audrey, taking his gloved hand in hers.

He guided her to the floor, his touch like a whisper

at the small of her back. She shivered as he took her into his arms.

"Here, you are cold." He pulled her shawl up around her shoulders.

"Thank you, my lord," said Audrey, her eyes studying the intricate folds of his cravat.

"Do you think the weather will permit us to have our drive this week?" he asked.

"I . . . I hope so, my lord."

"You know, Miss Langston, it is really not necessary to address me as 'my lord' constantly. You may call me Middlehurst. Or, when we are private"—he smiled as she looked around at the other dancers—"perhaps not private, but I didn't wish to put you to the blush by calling our waltz an intimate exchange."

"You are most considerate, Middlehurst," said Audrey, looking up at him.

"What I was going to say, Audrey, is that you might call me Charles, under these circumstances."

"So I might," she answered with an enigmatic smile.

His response was an energetic turn that carried them the length of the floor. Audrey matched him step for step, their movements perfectly synchronized. Faster, then more slowly; Charles marveled at how light she was on her feet. The only flaw he could detect from their exertions was an endearing silvery lock of hair that worked itself loose from her elaborate coiffure. When the music finally stopped, he leaned closer, tucking it into place again.

Audrey's eyes strayed to his lips, so close to hers.

Charles, instead of releasing her, tightened his hold, pulling her closer.

"I say, Charles, why don't we make up the next set; I'll partner Miss Langston and you can partner Miss Kelsey. I warn you, she can dance circles around both of us!" said William.

Charles stepped back, dropping his hands. Reluctantly, he tore his eyes away from Audrey and smiled at Emmeline. Each time he and Audrey met, they shared a secret smile. She was really quite beautiful, and she didn't feel the need to make inane conversation. He could envision her in his future very easily.

Still, marriage was such a permanent arrangement. And what of Colette?

"Well, Charles, when are you going to speak to her father?" asked Sir William when they had returned to the carriage from escorting Emmeline and Audrey to their door.

Charles slumped against the velvet upholstery and shrugged his shoulders. "I don't know. When would I have the chance? You know I can't leave London right now. Not even for a day or two."

"There's always the uncle."

"I know, I know. I just don't want Audrey to feel that I am rushing her. She has given me no indication she would welcome an offer from me."

William laughed at his friend. "You weren't in the position of watching the two of you dance together tonight. It was as if you were made for each other."

"I danced with each of the young ladies tonight. I

don't recall Audrey swooning in my arms. And when I told her she could call me Charles, she only said she 'might.' And she didn't give me leave to use her name."

"She was merely being proper," said William reasonably.

"Perhaps, but it is more than that. There are other things to consider," Charles opined enigmatically.

"Such as?"

The image of the petite Colette invaded his thoughts, and Charles grumbled, "Never you mind, Will. Besides, it will keep. Miss Langston isn't going anywhere!"

Audrey sat on her bed, wide awake, waiting for her impetuous cousin to make an appearance. She was certain Emmeline would come; being unable to wait until morning to analyze their evening. As if on cue, the door was opened surreptitiously, and Emmeline poked her head inside.

"Still awake?"

"And waiting," said Audrey with a smile.

Emmeline walked sedately across the carpet, perching daintily on the side of the bed. Audrey's brow rose in surprise.

"Did you enjoy yourself tonight?" asked her cousin.

"Very much so," said Audrey. "Middlehurst is such a fine host, and such a graceful dancer."

Emmeline essayed a distracted smile.

"Did you enjoy yourself?" prompted Audrey.

"Well, yes, I did. I did not expect to find the company so interesting," said Emmeline.

"The company? Or simply Sir William?" teased Audrey.

Emmeline looked over at Audrey, her expression serious. "He is very handsome, in a boyish, a gigantic boyish, sort of way." Emmeline shook her head, causing her long dark curls to ripple across her right shoulder. "He is also amusing."

"I can see you were quite captivated," said Audrey.

Emmeline grinned and wagged her finger at her cousin. "Now, none of that. We are supposed to be discussing you and Middlehurst. Did he come up to scratch? Or do you think he is going to?"

Audrey sat forward, hugging her knees. "I don't know. He hasn't mentioned the betrothal since that first night at Almack's when he quite took me by surprise. He never did say whether he was in favor of it or not. And now, perhaps he has forgotten all about it." Audrey's eyes begged for reassurance, and Emmeline moved closer and hugged her energetically.

"A man doesn't simply forget a betrothal. I think he is simply being polite. But the question is, when he does ask for your hand, will you accept him?"

Her gaze dreamy, Audrey seemed to look through Emmeline as she said quietly, "Yes, I'll accept. I'm afraid I am quite head over heels about him. Charles, that is. He has asked me to call him Charles."

"And will you?" asked Emmeline.

"I think I shall," said Audrey.

Five

Audrey submitted to the abigail's ministrations in silence. Stepping out of the blue silk gown, she caught a glimpse of her face in the mirror.

No wonder Millie is so quiet, she thought. I am looking very pathetic.

With a concerted effort, she put a smile on her face, saying, "You can go to bed now, Millie. I can brush out my hair."

"Thank you, miss. I'll just put this gown away."

When Audrey was alone, she sat down at the dressing table and pulled the pins from her hair. The heavy tresses cascaded around her shoulders.

"A pretty picture you make," she told her image. "And all because his lordship didn't put in an appearance at Almack's. I thought you knew better than to wear your heart on your sleeve."

But I have never been in love before, she told herself.

Audrey climbed into bed, pulling up the cover to wait for Emmeline's entrance; she waited in vain. Finally, she blew out the candles and turned over.

When the clock chimed three, Audrey reminded

herself once again of the futility of expecting to find a love match in an arranged marriage. The effect of this counsel was much the same as before. She heard the clock sound the next hour before exhaustion took its toll and released her to sleep.

Charles looked up from his morning coffee, blinking his red eyes before Sir William came into focus.

"Hullo, Will," he said wearily, returning his attention to the morning mail.

"Charles," said William, helping himself at the sideboard. He glanced over his shoulder at his friend, shaking his head slightly. "Haven't seen you since Vauxhall last Tuesday. Turned into a hermit, have you?"

"It has been a harrowing week; had a fire in the kitchens at the restaurant. We were able to put it out before it could spread, but we had to close for the night to clear the smoke."

"Ah, then that accounts for Wednesday. I think you should look at the calendar, Charles. It's Monday."

Charles let the invitation he was reading fall onto the polished surface of the table and looked up sharply. Sir William ignored his scrutiny and applied himself to his breakfast.

"Keeping tabs on me, Will?" drawled Charles.

Green eyes met blue, locked in a silent struggle. William grinned and shook his head.

"I know you couldn't care less about appearances, Charles, but you might give some consideration to Miss Langston's feelings."

"I don't believe I have done anything to warrant

your censure, William, but I will overlook your interference for the moment. How is it you are acquainted with Miss Langston's feelings?"

"I have it on the best authority that Miss Langston is decidedly miffed at your continued absence."

Charles grinned. "Miffed, is she? Now, I wonder where on earth you came by such a description. I had no idea your vocabulary was so varied."

"All right, all right. It was Miss Kelsey who told me your Miss Langston was miffed. To be quite truthful, Charles, I couldn't tell she was pining away over you at all. I mean, she is quite a beautiful young lady; she never lacks for partners at the balls. She even plays a good game of silver loo."

"Silver loo? Don't tell me you have been playing at silver loo! I hope no one from the club saw you. They'll revoke your membership!"

"I only play to please the ladies," said Will, turning a ruddy color to match his hair. "At least I am doing the pretty by them."

"Good. You continue to do the pretty; keep an eye on Miss Langston for me."

"That is not the way to win your betrothed," said William.

With his brows raised in disdain, Charles retorted, "I wasn't aware I needed to court Miss Langston. I merely need to make time to speak to her uncle."

"So you have decided to have her?"

"I suppose so. Miss Langston is an excellent choice. She will be a fine hostess; she knows how to run a large household, and she is heiress to a fine property which marches with Drake's tomb. In addition, her house is actually fit to live in. So, yes, she will make an admirable countess for me."

"God help her," muttered William.

"Beg pardon?"

"I can see her life is going to be full of warmth and affection," said Sir William, rising and striding to the door. "You'll have your restaurant, but what is going to keep her warm at night? You're a bloody fool, Charles. And if Miss Langston accepts you, then so is she!"

Charles scowled as the door slammed shut. What the deuce is he about, calling me a fool? he asked himself. And what's all this talk about Audrey keeping warm at night? Devil take him!

Charles shoved away from the table and stalked out of the room, striding down the hall and into his library. Sitting down at the desk, he pulled out paper and pen. Though he dipped the point into the ink, it dried before he could apply it to the paper. Dipping it again, he wrote:

Dear Miss Langston,

With a grumble, he tore up the sheet of paper and started again:

My Dear Audrey,

"Devil take it!"

My Dear Miss Langston,
   I must apologize for not taking pen in hand sooner, but

Charles put the pen down. What could he say? He certainly couldn't tell her that he couldn't call because his restaurant had nearly burned to the ground. Nor could he tell her that he simply hadn't been sure he wanted to see her again when the proximity of the lovely Colette was such a constant reminder of how wonderful the life of a bachelor could be.

But he had told William he would wed Miss Langston. She was beautiful, too, even if her beauty reminded him of a cold, winter day. And she was so demmed proper, not at all like the easygoing Colette.

But he couldn't wed Colette. Not that he really liked that idea either. Rimbeau might have been some minor sort of gentry in France, but he and his daughter were still French. It just wouldn't do to marry so far beneath his station.

With a grunt, Charles tore up the letter and began one more time:

Dear Audrey,

I hope you will forgive my not calling, but I have had pressing business matters to attend to. I hope you will honor me with a drive in the park this afternoon. I will call at five o'clock; if you are at home, I will know your reply.

Yr servant,
Middlehurst

Audrey tapped the folded note against her palm. Her first instinct was to send Middlehurst about his own business, though not in such inelegant terms, of course. But she knew she couldn't do that. Nor did she really want to do so. She couldn't fool herself that all her gaiety at the balls hadn't been forced. She knew better.

She crossed the chamber and opened the door that adjoined it to the dressing room. I will wear the plum-colored carriage dress, she thought, the one with the dashing new bonnet. If that had no effect on the handsome earl, then she would simply give up and set about forgetting his very existence!

She rang for Millie and began undoing the buttons on her morning gown.

"You rang, miss?"

"Yes, Millie. I would like a bath drawn. And let's try that new lavender scent I bought at Bartholomew's market."

"Very good, miss," said the abigail, smiling back at her mistress.

Three hours later, dressed in her elegant carriage dress, her bonnet's feather curling toward her chin at precisely the most bewitching point, Audrey congratulated herself on having accepted the earl's invitation. Charles, equally polished in a navy coat of superfine and fawn-colored breeches, set out to charm her.

"William, you see, lives up to that fiery red hair," he confided, offering only the briefest nod as Lord Asherton drove past before returning his full attention to her.

"You mean he has a temper?" asked Audrey.

"A temper? Why, that word is unequal to the task of describing his ire when he is crossed. He is usually the gentlest of souls, I assure you, but just let a bully try to intimidate some weak creature, and William will charge right in, tearing that bully limb to limb, if you will pardon such an expression. We were only nine, you will remember."

"Of course," said Audrey, laughing at the picture Charles painted of his old friend. "And in what role were you cast, Middlehurst? Bully or weakling?" she asked, her eyes wide with innocence.

Charles studied her suspiciously, spied the twinkle in her eyes and laughed. "I was neither, actually. I merely picked up the pieces afterward. That was usually when the schoolmasters arrived, and they would haul me away with William for our punishment."

"But you always stood by him," said Audrey, her features softening as she regarded him intently.

"Always," said Charles, blithely unaware that his schoolboy tales had added to his consequence in Audrey's eyes.

"And what about you, Audrey? Were you the scholar or the rebel at school?"

"I? I was neither. I enjoyed school, especially after Emmeline was old enough to join me. But I was never a ringleader. I was usually the one who cautioned everyone about what would happen when Miss Higginbotham found us out."

"But you went along anyway."

Audrey nodded, saying, "And I was usually blamed since I was two years older than Emmeline. She is the one who was the real leader; she still is."

Their conversation had so engrossed Audrey that

she hadn't realized they were quite off the beaten path, safely isolated from prying eyes.

Charles pulled back on the ribbons, bringing his well-mannered cattle to a halt. He put on the brake and wrapped the ribbons around it before turning to face her.

"Audrey, I had decided to speak to your uncle, but then I thought that would be unfair until I had spoken to you. I know there is a long-standing agreement between our families, but I would be loath to entrap you by that. I . . . I suppose I'm asking if you would like to marry me." He took a deep breath and exhaled loudly.

Audrey did not notice; she was caught up in her own thoughts. Does he love me? No, of course not. He is only doing what is expected of him. But he must have some regard for me, she told herself desperately. He was not under any constraint to make me an offer. Not really.

"Audrey?" said Charles, suddenly gone white. Was she about to refuse him? he wondered, his thoughts flying to William's admonition that morning.

Audrey left her twisted doubts behind and looked up, studying his face, his dear face, carefully. What she read there made up her mind, and she smiled at him.

"Yes, Charles, I would very much like to marry you."

Relief flooded over him, and Charles smiled broadly. He lifted her hand in his and kissed her knuckles.

"Good, good," was all he could manage. Picking

up the reins, he threw off the brake, sending the carriage forward again. As they returned to Rotten Row, Charles became businesslike and said, "I will call on your uncle in the morning. I must attend to other business this afternoon and evening. Will you be home tomorrow?"

"Yes, Charles," she said softly, deflated by his brisk manner.

"Good, then perhaps they will allow us a few moments alone together. Do you go to the Petersons' ball tomorrow night?"

"I think so."

"I suppose I could just see you there, in which case, there would be no need for you to wait all day for me to call."

They had arrived back at her uncle's town house, and Charles excused himself from accompanying her to the door on account of his horses since he had not brought along his tiger. With a forced smile, Audrey bade him good-bye and hopped down. She looked up, hoping for something, perhaps a fond farewell.

Instead, Charles looked at his watch. Snapping it shut and slapping the reins vigorously, he rolled quickly out of sight, congratulating himself on a job well done. He had been right to choose Audrey Langston; she was all that was proper and seemly.

Had he been privy to the scene that ensued, the Earl of Middlehurst would have been astounded at the profundity of passion his betrothed betrayed. Entering the house, Audrey said not a word to the stoic Beamish.

Sweeping up the stairs, she entered Emmeline's chamber, closing the door carefully before turning and saying through clenched teeth, "I hope my father will be satisfied! I am going to marry the beast!"

Emmeline threw aside the latest copy of *La Belle Assemblée* she had been perusing and squealed with glee. She jumped up, hugged Audrey and pulled her toward the sofa.

"How wonderful, Audrey! Tell me all about it!"

Audrey turned a baleful glare on her cousin, rose, and walked to the other side of the chamber. Turning, she demanded, "Did you not hear what I said? I am marrying a beast!"

"Beast? Middlehurst? You must be joking, Aude. You're in love with him!"

Ignoring this last, Audrey said, "Joking? Not I."

"What did he do?" demanded Emmeline, her own righteous indignation growing by the moment.

Always ready to do battle for others, Audrey thought fleetingly; really, Emmeline and Sir William should make a match of it. But she shook these thoughts aside.

"It is not any one thing, but all of them put together. I didn't even realize what a beast he was until after I had accepted him."

"Then we shall tell Papa to refuse him for you!"

"I can't do that!"

"You can't marry a beast!" declared Emmeline.

"Oh, I don't know what to do!" wailed Audrey, angry tears threatening to spill across her lower lashes.

Emmeline coaxed her back to the sofa. Patting her cousin's hand, she asked, "Can you talk about it?"

Audrey nodded and began bravely, "First there was the matter of my new bonnet." Emmeline waited silently, and Audrey announced, "He didn't even comment on it."

Emmeline looked puzzled, but she refrained from passing judgment. "Go on," she said.

"Then he tried to endear himself to me by telling outrageous stories of his school days."

"That, surely, is not so terrible."

Audrey raised her brow and pursed her lips. "Then he drove away from the crowds of people until we were quite alone."

"Oh, Audrey," breathed Emmeline, uncertain what might have happened, but having been warned of such evil by Riggs, she was fully prepared to hear the worst.

"He asked me to marry him."

"And then he . . ."

"Well, he kissed my hand."

"And then . . ."

"And then he drove me home! He didn't even help me to the door. Oh, and he made some excuse about not seeing me tomorrow until the Petersons' ball. Something about not wanting me to have to wait on him tomorrow, as if I would! It is the outside of enough!" Audrey finished, her eyes narrowing at the memory.

Emmeline's bowed head gave Audrey no indication of her listener's opinion, so she goaded her, saying, "Well, don't you think that is beastly?"

First, Emmeline laughed out loud, then silently, her shoulders shaking between each gasp for air.

Audrey rose and stalked to the door.

"Don't go, Aude," managed Emmeline, weakly extending a hand to bade her cousin to remain.

"I shall speak to you later, when you have remembered your manners!" declared Audrey, slipping outside.

Marching to her own room, she stopped in front of the chevel glass, studying her image for a few seconds before tearing the offending bonnet from her head and throwing it to the floor. Lips still pursed, Audrey moved to the bed and, with a whoosh of sound, fell backward, staring in silence at the canopy of lace.

She wasn't wrong, she told herself fiercely. Middlehurst had been a beast, offering for her and then leaving her at the door. He hadn't been the least bit lovelorn, begging permission to see her, to be with her. He certainly hadn't resembled the heroes in the tales of romance she had read.

All he cares for is his consequence, she thought. She might as well be a mare at Tattersall's. She was just convenient. She was there, suitable, and obviously available since her father had seen fit to remind him of the connection.

My father! she silently exclaimed, turning over and staring into space. Middlehurst was just another man such as her father. All they really cared for were estates, suitable matches, and settlements.

Audrey closed her eyes, picturing his face when she had accepted him. He had smiled, his handsome face lighting with pleasure. Or perhaps it had just been relief at having the thing done and over with. What a lowering notion that was, Audrey reflected.

But he did offer for you, a tiny voice mentioned in her ear. He must care for you a little; he must. He is not desperate for a wife; he has no pressing need for one.

Her lips curved into a smile as Audrey chose to listen to that voice; stretching deliciously, she embraced this thought: he does care.

"Rimbeau, a word with you, in my office. Colette, you also, if you please."

When the door had closed, and Charles was facing his two employees, he wondered briefly what it was he wished to say. He didn't really have to inform them of his coming nuptials. I don't owe it to them, he thought, as he looked first at Rimbeau and then at the seductive girl.

Clearing his throat uncomfortably, Charles said quickly, "I wanted you to know that I am betrothed, so I may find it difficult to spend as much time here at the restaurant as I have been."

"Congratulations, my lord," said Rimbeau.

Charles shot him a warning glance, and Colette said sharply, "There is no need to dissemble, my lord earl. I have long since guessed your identity; I did not need my father to tell me."

"I see," said Charles. "Then you do not find it odd that I choose to spend my days here cooking?"

"A man may do what he pleases with his time, my

lord. A woman, ah, that is different. But for me, I am very pleased to be here, working for you. I would not wish anyone to discover your secret when it might jeopardize my position. Your secret is my secret," she said proudly.

"Thank you, Colette. I thought you suspected; you are much too clever to cozen. Well, that is all I needed to say. I have never been betrothed before, of course, but it seems to me the fellows have to dance attendance on their fiancées a great deal of the time," said Charles, thinking out loud.

Rimbeau laughed, saying, "But that is what young lovers wish to do, *oui*, my lord? They want only to be near the one they love, eh?"

"Yes, yes, I suppose so. But things in this country are not as they are in yours, Rimbeau. Here, we marry for money, estates, or position. Love is secondary," said Charles.

Rimbeau shook his head in stupefaction, "Ah, the English, you go about things so strangely."

Colette, who had been silently studying the earl, rose and said briskly, "We must return to work. A Mr. Parnell has reserved the private parlor for sixteen tomorrow night. I must make certain we have enough pheasant for his party."

Her father preceded her, returning to the kitchen; Colette paused at the door.

"If you find that you are bored by the, uh, entertainments of Society, my lord, you must not hesitate to return to us here. We . . . I shall miss you," she added, blinking slowly as if fighting tears.

"Thank you, Colette. I shall remember that," said

Charles, wondering what it was about this girl's manner which made him forget everything else. Nodding, she turned away; he watched her as she crossed the bustling kitchen to the dining-room door through which she disappeared.

Charles took a deep breath, the first in several seconds. He shook his head thoughtfully. Their beauty was completely opposite, and Colette was no prettier than Audrey. Perhaps it was not her beauty but her sensuality which attracted him to her. She had a way of looking at a man that drew him in like a moth to a candle's flame.

He would have to be careful, he thought. Colette was not one he wanted trouble with, not with her hot temper. He had seen her reduce one of the pot boys to tears in seconds with a fiery scold. After witnessing that episode, Charles had decided he never wanted to cause her to rebuke him.

Turning, he made his way outside, climbed into the hansom cab, and signaled Handie to take him home. Instead of entering the garden, however, Charles went to the stables, surprising his tiger by his stealthy entrance.

"Cor, my lord, you do give a fellow a start, don't you?"

"How restive is my gelding?" asked Charles, ignoring his ever-complaining servant.

"Too much for town, I'm thinking. I exercised the bays this morning. Took 'em out on the Richmond road."

"Very well, then make it the bays. You may accom-

pany me; I've got an errand to do in town, and I'll
need you to hold the horses."

"I don't know why I'm taking such pains with my
toilette," said Audrey haughtily. "Middlehurst probably won't even put in an appearance."

Emmeline studied the effect of the topaz stones
against her cousin's gown and shook her head. "The
pearls are definitely better," she said, handing these
to Millie to place around her mistress's neck.

Standing back, she nodded, saying, "You are taking
such pains because he is your betrothed, and you
want him to know what he is missing every time he
does not have the opportunity to see you. I must say,"
she added when Audrey had risen and been helped
into her gown of alabaster silk, "you are looking very
beautiful tonight. It must be because you are a
bride." Emmeline laughed at her wit, and Audrey
frowned.

"You are being absurd," said Audrey, but she admitted privately she was in looks that night.

Emmeline, standing just behind her, tugged at the
sprig muslin she was sporting and frowned at her
image. "You are simply spoiled," she grumbled. "If
I were half so tall and elegant, I would want nothing
else in the world. You should try being short and
pudgy for a while."

"You are not pudgy. You have slimmed down very
nicely," said Audrey.

"For the Season. But I know I will never be considered elegant. That is why I must strive for outra-

geous without stepping too far outside the social boundaries"

"You have your following, Emmeline. You know you never lack for partners"

"Oh, I know, Aude. And truly, I don't wish to complain. I am very happy being friends with every young man in London. Well, not *every* young man. I think I frighten the dandies and fops." She laughed.

"True, you number among your set only the neck or nothing Corinthians. How many members of the Four-in-Hand Club are courting you now?" asked Audrey.

Emmeline laughed. "You know just what to say to cheer me. Of course, there is one member who is not courting me."

"Sir William? Then perhaps you can explain why he has coincidentally appeared at every dull musicale, card party, rout, and ball we have attended in the past week?" demanded Audrey. "And well you should blush, Miss Emmeline Kelsey. The poor man is obviously head over heels. Now, let us go downstairs and collect Riggs. You know she has been waiting this age. She says if the Petersons' pastries are not to be missed, one must arrive early and begin tucking them away before too many guests arrive!"

Mr. and Mrs. Peterson were known for their lavish entertainments. They were not, however, overly discriminating in their choice of guests. Everyone who had any claim to distinction was sent a card, and everyone invariably showed up.

In keeping with Mr. Peterson's travels to the West Indies where he owned a plantation, this year's theme was a tropical island. Hot-house plants filled every corner. A garden of tropical orchids bloomed in the dining room. The food, though not reminiscent of the West Indies, did boast a roasted pig, and the punch was orange colored, with floating blossoms and fruit.

Mr. Peterson wore a white suit of clothes and Mrs. Peterson, a large woman, wore a bright blue gown with flowers tucked here and there. They stood on the threshold of the grand ballroom, greeting their guests genially.

"Good evening, Miss Riggs, young ladies. I hope you'll find visiting our little island a pleasure this evening," said the convivial Mr. Peterson, pressing Miss Riggs's hand warmly while his wife was engaged in greeting the next guests in line. Riggs mumbled some platitude and moved hurriedly along.

Winking at Audrey, Emmeline whispered, "Mr. Peterson almost married our Riggs, you know."

"Emmeline! You will never go to heaven if you tell such farradiddles!" exclaimed the indignant spinster.

"You see how defensive she gets; one wonders if there are still a few embers burning."

"Methinks the lady doth protest too much," added Audrey.

"Humph!" said Riggs, turning away with a rosy blush.

This gave Emmeline the opportunity to send one or two flirtatious smiles to various gentlemen before

Riggs announced disdainfully that she would go and search out those pastries.

"There is Sir William," whispered Emmeline.

Audrey nodded, smiling when she caught Sir William's eye. He hurried forward, bowing elegantly before them. Now it was Emmeline's turn to blush, leaving Audrey to step into the breach and greet Sir William for them both.

"Isn't this a marvel, Sir William? Have you ever seen anything so . . . untamed?" said Audrey.

"I might have done," said William, smiling down at Emmeline before adding politely, "The Petersons have outdone themselves. I understand last year it was a pirate's cove."

"It was positively gloomy," said Emmeline. "I like this much better. The flowers are lovely. My mother has a green thumb; she has a wonderful rose garden at home. In the summer, the fragrance is heavenly."

"And did you inherit her green thumb?" asked William.

"No, but I did inherit the most uncanny ability to hire the very best people," she said, glancing up at Sir William through long lashes.

"A most underrated talent," he replied. "Might I procure some refreshments for you ladies?"

"Not right now," said Audrey, looking past him, searching the ballroom for some sign of her fiancé. She grimaced at the thought. A fine thing, having a fiancé without having spoken to him since they had become officially betrothed.

Finally, not spying him in the multitude, Audrey

asked casually, "Did Middlehurst come with you this evening?"

"No, he said he would meet me here. I don't know if I'm supposed to mention it, but I understand I should extend my best wishes to you. He's a lucky fellow."

"Thank you, Sir William," said Audrey.

Emmeline pursed her lips and said outrageously, "He's a bacon-brained clodpole, if you ask me!"

"Emmeline, such language!"

Sir William's booming laugh attracted the attention of others, but he didn't seem to care, saying, "You have an endearing honesty about you, my dear. The man can be a real clodpole. Oh, sorry, Miss Langston, but Charles is a very old friend of mine. Why he has not yet put in an appearance tonight, swept you off your feet, or at the very least onto the dance floor, is beyond me. But there you have it. Charles never does what one would expect of him. He was always shocking his fellow officers with some prank or other. The worst, I suppose, was his damn . . . er . . . infernal cooking. I thought his batman would explode with indignation when Charles threw him out of our makeshift kitchen. I remember . . . Well, that's neither here nor there," he added, grinning sheepishly.

"I'm sure it is something important that has kept Middlehurst away," said Emmeline.

Both ladies turned expectantly when Sir William seemed to have something caught in his throat. But he merely coughed and looked away.

"Here is Mr. Parnell, a particular friend of mine.

Parnell, didn't know if you would be here or not. Thought you were celebrating someone's birthday or something."

"I am, but not until later in the week. Having supper at Chez Canard on Wednesday, don't you know. I see you have secured the company of the two loveliest creatures here tonight," he added gallantly.

"Miss Langston, Miss Kelsey, may I present Mr. Parnell. He was on the Peninsula with me and Charles."

"Charmed, ladies," said the young man with an elegant bow. "Listen, they're tuning up for a waltz. Miss Langston, won't you do me the honor?"

"I would love to, Mr. Parnell," said Audrey, determined once again to have a wonderful evening without her new fiancé.

Sir William led Emmeline onto the floor, giving Audrey the satisfaction of knowing that one of them was enjoying herself. Mr. Parnell was agreeable, but his touch did not send anything dancing up and down her spine.

Sir William claimed the second dance, and remained by her side when she declared she would sit out the third. He set about charming her, along with his friend Lord Asherton. But by the end of the third set, Audrey was in high dudgeon. It was all she could do to keep a polite mask in place. Finally, she sought refuge in the ladies' withdrawing room.

As she was returning to the ballroom, Charles appeared, stepping into her path so that she could not ignore his presence. Audrey told herself to disregard how utterly handsome he appeared in his evening clothes, with his boyish smile, his hair looking wind-blown, and on top of all that, short of breath, sup-posedly from hurrying to her side.

"Good evening, Middlehurst," she said tautly.

"Good evening, my dear. Seems I am never on time; a particular fault of mine, I'm afraid. Am I in your black books?" His smile was calculated to tease her out of her pique.

"Why on earth would you be in my black books?" she asked, her nose in the air.

Charles laughed and took her hand in his, pulling her down the empty corridor until they were alone.

Audrey fought the butterflies that had taken flight when he touched her, but all she could manage to say was a breathless, "I should be returning to the ballroom. Riggs will be looking for me."

"In a moment. Won't you accept my apology?" he asked. "I know I should have been here earlier; I should probably have escorted you. But I did have an errand, and it took longer than I had thought."

"It is no concern of mine. . . . What's this?" asked Audrey. Charles took her hand in his and placed a long, slender box in her palm.

"Open it."

She hesitated, fighting the petty impulse to throw it in his face. Curiosity won out, and she opened it with a quick intake of breath as the candlelight glit-tered on the bright jewels.

"Oh, Charles, they are lovely. And the sapphire is magnificent."

"I'm glad you like them," he said, taking the strand of pearls and turning her. He removed the short strand that she was wearing, dropping it into the box before fastening the new necklace around her slender neck. Turning her again, he stepped back to admire her.

"You have improved them greatly." He glanced around, spying a mirror in the hall. "Look," he said.

Audrey gazed at the lustrous strand of perfectly matched pearls. In its center, hanging just above her décolletage, was a shimmering sapphire surrounded by diamonds. She looked beyond her image into Charles's face, and smiled.

"Thank you, Charles," she said, rotating in his arms to face him.

His eyes caressed her lips for a moment before he kissed her. Audrey's lids drooped as she savored the giddy sensation of his touch. His lips were warm and gentle; she put a tentative hand on his broad chest. Then he stepped away. He straightened the pendant, the tips of his fingers grazing her breasts and causing her heart to beat erratically.

Then, unaccountably, Audrey's mind was pulled back home to Cook's apricot tarts, and the spell was broken. Shaking her head, she cleared her senses.

"I wanted you to have them," said Charles. "The pearls are new, but the sapphire and diamond pendant are part of the Middlehurst jewels."

He took her hand and tucked it into the crook of his arm, guiding her back to the lights of the ballroom.

"You must be prepared for people's reactions. The sapphire is well known; everyone will instantly realize that we are betrothed. There's no turning back now," he added, gazing down at her with apparent affection.

"I had no thought of turning back, Charles," said Audrey, returning his smile.

She was unprepared, however, as they entered the "tropical" ballroom and all the guests turned, agog with curiosity, their eyes glued to her breasts. No one, of course, asked outright about her new necklace as they made their way through the crowd, but the speculation in those gazes was palpable.

"You weren't joking, were you, Charles?" commented Audrey as he swept her into a waltz that was just beginning.

Tightening his hold on her, Charles smiled at her use of his given name. He had always thought Charles such a commonplace choice, but Audrey's voice made it sound singularly majestic.

"I daresay half the guests present, being male, would enjoy staring at you in any case, but I think it safe to say the ladies are interested only in the necklace."

"And what it represents. You are considered quite a prize on the matrimonial market."

"I? I don't think so. I hardly ever attend these things; I am most unobliging in social matters."

"You underrate yourself," said Audrey. "I find you very obliging. You are a wonderful dancer and your manners are impeccable."

"Thank you so much, schoolmistress Audrey," said Charles, laughing.

With a deliberately lecherous study of her lips, he

continued to twirl her about the room. Audrey felt her face grow warm, her limbs weak.

"Stop that," she whispered finally.

"But I find contemplating your mouth very fulfilling," he said outrageously. "Were we alone. . . ."

"Then perhaps it is best we are not," Audrey chided primly as the music came to an end.

Six

"You caused quite a stir tonight," said Emmeline when she had settled under the coverlet of Audrey's bed.

Audrey smiled contentedly. "You mean because of the necklace."

"That, and the other thing, too," said Emmeline, her dark eyes dancing with mischief.

"What other thing?" asked Audrey, chiding herself privately for rising to the bait as usual. If only once she could ignore Emmeline's cryptic comments, she felt sure she would never again have to listen to her gossip.

"At first, I was quite jealous," said Emmeline, warming to the topic when she saw Audrey's puzzled frown. "Yes, I mean, you knew that Sir William was the object of my interest, and yet you still managed to monopolize his time quite shamelessly."

Audrey leaned back against her pillows and said indignantly, "That is the outside of enough! I hardly spoke to Sir William after the first two hours!"

"But it was those first two hours which had everyone talking. There you were looking rather down in the mouth, and there was Sir William, ministering to your every whim."

"Fustian! He danced with me once—a country dance, at that!"

"And he sat out the next dance with you."

"But I was tired," protested Audrey. "And Lord Asherton was there, too! Emmeline, surely you don't think . . . I would never . . ." Audrey stopped when Emmeline bent over with laughter.

"You are incorrigible!" she snapped.

When Emmeline had regained her voice, she apologized. "Audrey, really, I never thought you were trying to turn Sir William's head. I was only joking."

"Well, I'm glad you know I would never do that," Audrey told her cousin.

Sobering, Emmeline said seriously, "But there were remarks I overheard, Audrey. Some people, mostly the old tabbies, were wondering why you were wearing the Middlehurst jewels when you had been so familiar with Sir William."

Audrey sighed. "It is all so tiring, Emmeline. You cannot even be a friend without someone tattling that you are fast. Now I shall have to take pains to be sure I am never alone with Sir William, even at a ball."

"I have been thinking, Aude," said Emmeline.

"Uh-oh, I think I shall blow out the light," said Audrey.

"No, no. It is just . . . I don't know how to say this without offending you, so I will simply come out and say it. I think it would be no bad thing if *some people* thought you were enamored of Sir William."

"*Some people?*"

"Yes, like Middlehurst. Audrey, I cannot turn a blind eye on the wretched manner he has of ignoring you. Why, you dressed expressly for him this morning, waiting to be summoned to the library after his talk with Papa. Instead, off he goes to his club, or some such place, without so much as a cuddle or a kiss!"

"Emmeline!"

"And you needn't act the prude with me! I know you read those penny-press romance novels. I know you would not find a kiss from your fiancé amiss!"

"Nevertheless, one simply doesn't talk about it!" said Audrey, blushing as she remembered Charles's kiss.

Emmeline regarded her with narrowed eyes and exclaimed, "Aha! So he has kissed you!"

"That is none of your business, Emmeline," said Audrey, blowing out the candles and settling into bed, hoping her cousin would take the hint and leave her alone.

There was still the light from the small fire, and Emmeline was not so easily deterred. "No, no, it isn't any of my business, but I'm glad to know it. I won't worry about you so."

Audrey patted her cousin's hand. "Thank you for worrying, Emmeline. But truly, I am quite content with this betrothal. He is not very attentive, but he makes up for it when I do see him."

"Very well, if you are happy, then I shall try to be also. But if you should wish for Sir William to make him jealous, just let me know."

"And are you and Sir William so close that you

could make such an impertinent request?'' demanded Audrey, hoping to turn the tables on her cousin.

But Emmeline would not be deterred, saying, "Never mind that. Just tell me, and I'll take care of it.''

"Certainly not, Emmeline. It would be dishonest.''

"All's fair in love and war,'' said the younger cousin. "But I shan't say anything.''

A companionable silence fell between them; then Emmeline asked quietly, "What was it like, his kiss? Did it make you want to swoon?''

Audrey chuckled and then said thoughtfully, "It was quite pleasant. But it was really rather odd, too; for some reason, it brought to mind Cook's apricot tarts.''

Audrey glanced down at her cousin's surprised expression, and both young ladies fell into whoops.

The announcement appeared in the *Post* the next morning; Audrey was occupied all day with calls from well-wishers and the curious. Charles had been right about the necklace; all congratulated themselves on having guessed the secret betimes.

Audrey tried to ignore the subtle jibes about Charles's absence that afternoon, but the arrows hit home. Sir William was present, his quick wit saving her several times from inquiries which were too uncomfortable. These inquiries were followed closely by pitying glances around the bustling salon.

"Never mind,'' said Emmeline, keeping her husky

voice as low as possible. "You are bound to see him at Almack's tonight."

"He did promise me he would attend," said Sir William, his voice also lowered.

His huge hand covered Audrey's briefly, and she smiled. The trio turned as one; they could almost feel the interested stares.

Sir William shifted uncomfortably in his chair and said, "Miss Kelsey, perhaps we could go for that drive now?"

Cocking her head to one side, Emmeline indicated Audrey. Sir William took the hint instantly.

"And Miss Langston, would you care to accompany us?" he asked. Emmeline favored him with a wide smile.

"Do come, Audrey," she said hurriedly, seeing that her cousin was on the verge of declining. "I would think you have put up with sufficient company for now. Mama would agree, too."

"Yes, you run along," Riggs, who was shamelessly eavesdropping on their conversation, urged.

"If you truly don't mind, Sir William. I would love an outing," said Audrey.

"I would consider myself the luckiest of men to have two such beautiful ladies gracing my carriage," he declared, rising as they did and bowing slightly.

"Read about your betrothal in the paper, Charles," said Mr. Parnell when he encountered the earl at White's that afternoon. "I suppose congratulations are in order?"

Charles, who had been at the restaurant all morning, nodded in distraction, wondering for a moment why Parnell had phrased his felicitation as a question.

"Thank you," he said. "Have you seen Compton?"

Parnell snickered. "Not here."

"Where the deuce is he? He was to meet me here at five o'clock," said Charles.

Again that snicker. "Saw him not above two hours ago at the Kelsey town house."

Mistaking the reason for Parnell's amusement, Charles laughed and said, "Who would have thought old Will would end up in the petticoat line?"

"Seems to be taking to it," said Parnell. "Surprised, though, that you don't seem to mind," he added.

Charles frowned. "Why the devil should I mind?"

"Nothing, nothing," said Parnell, backing away. "It's none of my business, none at all. If you'll excuse me . . . ?"

Charles waved him away. Calling for a glass and a bottle of Madeira, he found a quiet nook and picked up the newspaper. His long hours of work and play caught up with him, and he nodded off.

Some time later, Charles awoke with a start. He recognized Parnell's voice with no trouble.

"I tell you, there he was, bigger than life—which he is anyway—cozying up to the Langston chit."

"Shhh! Someone will hear you."

"Doesn't matter. I spoke to Middlehurst; he has no idea what is toward. Either that, or he simply doesn't care," said Parnell.

"Surely he cares. How could a man not care if he's

cuckolded before he is even wed," said the other man whose voice Charles could not place.

Charles rose from his chair, flexing his powerful neck and shoulder muscles as he stared at the two speakers. Parnell blanched; the other man, stocky Squire Wentworth, faced him squarely.

"Know you must be wanting to plant me and Parnell a facer, my lord, but there's no need for that. Only saying what we know to be true. Seems to me, it needs saying. If you don't know about the gel, then you—"

The man dropped to the ground, out cold. Parnell backed away, but Charles caught him by the collar.

"Come here, Parnell. You will tell me what the devil you and this country bumpkin were so engrossed about. If you have heard some gossip, you owe it to me to tell me. If you're lying and spreading gossip about my betrothed, I'll call you out."

"Here now, Charles, no need for that. Devil take me, you're too deuced deadly with sword and pistol! I don't want to be the one to tell you, but there are a few of the fellows who were commenting on the fact that Miss Langston—a delightful young lady, to be sure—seems to enjoy Sir William's company more than yours. I'm sure there is a logical explanation," added Parnell as the earl's fist clenched under his nose while his other hand lifted him off the floor by his collar.

"There is," growled Charles. "Will is looking after her while I am engaged in some pressing business concerns. That's all there is to it. Understand?"

"Of course, of course," said Parnell, relaxing as his

feet touched the floor again, and Charles loosened his grip.

"If anyone else says anything, Parnell, I count on you to set them straight."

"Of course, Charles. Be happy to, happy," stammered Parnell, moving out of his friend's reach. "Knew it was just a misunderstanding. Knew it."

Charles smiled tightly and nodded before leaving the club. His first instinct was to go to Audrey and demand an explanation. It infuriated him that her behavior had caused speculation at his club. And if the men were wagering on it, then the drawing rooms had to be bursting with the news.

Before he reached the Kelsey town house, however, he had thought better of it; he would speak to William instead. They had planned to dine at the club, but he knew Will would seek him out at home when he didn't put in an appearance. Very likely, Will would hear what he had done to the squire, and he would be ready with his explanation.

Charles ground his teeth. He hadn't asked Will to look after Audrey; he could only hope Will had decided on his own to help out. It would be disastrous if Will had formed a tendre for Audrey. Or worse, if she had formed one for Will.

Charles's fist clenched at the intolerable thought. He took the steps to his front door two at a time, but his stride was angry, not joyful. Frowning, he cleared the front hall of servants, growling at his butler to make sure the decanter was full in the library.

"Very good, my lord," said the butler. "Perhaps I

should inform you that your grandmother has come for a visit."

Charles turned very slowly, his store of patience exhausted "Of course she has. Twenty years without a visit to London, and now here she is. Where is she at this moment, Duncan?"

"She has called on Miss Langston, my lord," said the butler.

Charles nodded, shaking his head slightly.

"I did try to suggest that she might find a hotel more to her liking, my lord, but she wouldn't listen."

Charles waved his hand, dismissing such a possibility as too absurd for consideration. "She has never listened to anyone in her entire life, Duncan. Why would she start now?" Charles rallied a little, saying, "Just make certain you give her a chamber as far away from mine as possible."

"I have already done so, my lord."

Charles bypassed the library, judging that room too public to discourage his grandmother's entry. Continuing up the stairs to his chamber, he bolted the door when he was inside. His valet, who was laying out his evening clothes, looked alarmed, then knowing.

"Her ladyship did say she wished to accompany you to Almack's tonight, my lord. She was most specific about that."

"I do not doubt that, Higgins. You may as well draw my bath. I don't think she will barge in here without knocking, but one never knows," said Charles, beginning to strip off his clothes.

* * *

Audrey and Emmeline returned from their drive with Sir William in high spirits. Laughing, they entered the salon, thinking at first that it was empty.

"Sir William, you really mustn't tell us such naughty tales about the earl. After all, Audrey has to marry the fellow!" said Emmeline, her throaty voice as clear and boisterous as ever.

"Emmeline, Audrey," hissed Aunt Patricia urgently. "Come and meet Lady Middlehurst, Lord Middlehurst's grandmother."

Without missing a beat, Audrey turned and advanced toward the sofa near the front window. Lady Middlehurst, her blue eyes as sharp as a hawk's, studied her up and down as she made her best curtsy.

"Delighted to make your acquaintance, my lady."

Emmeline hurriedly curtseyed, her face uncomfortably red. "Delighted," she parroted.

"How do you do?" asked the dowager, a hint of a smile in her eyes. "That you, Will Compton?" she barked suddenly.

Will, who had been hanging back, rolled his eyes and came forward to bow over her plump hand.

"Didn't know you were coming to town, my lady," he said, stepping back again.

"That's because I didn't warn you . . . or that scapegrace grandson of mine either. Sit down, all of you. You are not in the presence of royalty!"

When the trio had complied, the dowager countess addressed Audrey. "You turned out much better than I expected, child. You were a distinctly gangly thing as a youngster."

"Thank you, my lady," said Audrey, looking down

hurriedly lest her future relative detect her amusement at these bizarre comments.

"How tall are you?"

"Five feet and eight inches, my lady."

The dowager grunted. "Good. You're just about up to Charles's weight then."

Audrey did look up at this, stiffening her posture and lifting her chin. "I am no milk-and-water-miss, if that is what you mean . . . my lady."

The dowager smiled for the first time, nodding her approval. "Good girl! I knew you would be the one for that grandson of mine. The Langston family has ever been proud and uncompromising. The first time I ever laid eyes on you, child, you were riding neck or nothing across a field. The next time, you were berating a footman for being cruel to the pot boy. Courage and compassion—an unconquerable combination."

Audrey turned pink at this praise and stammered, "Thank you. But when did you visit Drake's tomb? I mean, Drake's Manor?"

Her ladyship waved aside this awkwardness, saying, "It is a tomb, but it is my family seat, even if we no longer live there. But I saw you when Charles was sent down from school . . ." She focused her attention on Sir William who shifted uncomfortably in his chair. "Which time was that, *Sir* William?"

"I don't quite remember, my lady," he said.

"No, you wouldn't. You weren't there, were you? You had gone home to your parents where you belonged. Charles, however, thought to escape my wrath by hiding at the 'tomb.' That is when we ar-

ranged the marriage, Miss Langston, your parents
and I. I thought perhaps Charles had overlooked it,
but I see he has not completely forgotten his duty to
his name. However, I decided to come to town myself
to see that things progressed properly."

Audrey frowned. "So Charles did not write to you?"

"No need. I knew you were in town; I knew he was.
It was time. I understand from your aunt that the
announcement appeared in this morning's *Post.*"
Audrey nodded. "Then the boy has finally come to
his senses. It is high time he is married. And you,
too, for that matter. How old are you?" she demanded.

"Four and twenty," said Audrey, her expression
daring the old woman to make any further comment
about her age

But the dowager only cackled and said, "Good! Old
enough to be interesting, but not too old to give me
a basketful of great-grandchildren!"

"Would you care for some more tea, my lady?"
asked Aunt Patricia.

"No, no, I must be going. Haven't seen Charles
yet; can't wait to surprise him. It was a pleasure meeting you, Miss Langston, and your charming family,"
the dowager proclaimed.

"Thank you, my lady," said Audrey and her aunt.

The countess turned and commanded, "You, William, will accompany me back to the town house."

"Yes, my lady," said William, adding uncertainly,
"Are you staying with Charles?"

"Of course I am! Pray do not stand there gawking.
Say your farewells, and let us be gone!"

"Good day, my lady, Sir William," chorused the ladies.

"Good day," he said, bowing over Aunt Patricia's hand only to be called to heel by the dowager countess.

"I tell you, Charles, I won't be responsible for my actions if I am forced into company with her!"

Charles watched in amusement as his friend strode up and down the length of the chamber. They made a fine pair, he thought, dressed in knee breeches for Almack's and gone to ground like a pair of foxes.

"Be a man," said Charles, laughing. "You don't see me cringing in fear of an old woman."

Sir William stopped and faced his tormentor squarely. "First of all, I heard the lock turn before you could allow me entry into this chamber, so I know you are hiding from her yourself. Furthermore, she is not my cross to bear!"

"But I need your help," said Charles. "I can't possibly dance attendance on both Audrey and my grandmother without giving up my time at the restaurant."

"Then you'll just have to give up the blasted restaurant!" exclaimed his friend. "If it's the wager, we'll declare all bets off."

Charles shook his head. "It's not that easy. If I quit cooking now, the restaurant patrons will realize something has changed and try all the harder to discover the truth behind the place!"

"I don't care," said William. "Anything is preferable to spending time with your grandmother."

"Anything? Are you going to bury yourself in the country while she is in town? Do you truly think you can escape her wrath? I swear the woman will hunt you down. Who is it she will blame for encouraging me?" demanded Charles.

Sir William shivered at this. "I need a drink," he declared.

"That is the first logical thing either of us has said in the past half an hour," agreed Charles.

When they were settled in front of the fireplace, glasses in hand, they heaved a joint sigh of relief. Somehow, things didn't look quite so intolerable by the time they started on their second vessel. The clock struck nine and the door opened unceremoniously.

Higgins, Charles's valet stood back guiltily, the keys dangling from his waistcoat.

"I'm sorry, my lord."

"Don't blame him, Charles. Good heavens, you here, too, William? Well, I see you are both dressed appropriately. Shall we go?"

"By all means," said Charles, resigned to his fate.

When he reached the door, his grandmother looked him up and down, her gaze settling finally on his cravat.

"That's what you dandies are calling a cravat these days, eh?" William made a choking sound, and she added, "Oh, I know you're all tying them the same. I don't suppose anyone thinks anything about it."

Charles offered his arm to his grandmother, saying,

"I believe Will was having difficulty swallowing the label of dandy, Grandmother."

"Humph! Meant nothing by it, my boy. If it's any comfort to you, neither of you would have been labeled a dandy back in my day. But you are both quite presentable. A lady could do worse than to be escorted by the two of you."

Over her head, Charles and William exchanged quick glances of amazement.

Almack's glittered with the jewels of the Ton. The patronesses bestowed the coveted vouchers on only the *crème de la crème.* The disappointment of never receiving vouchers was devastating; the shame of having them withdrawn was an obstacle not to be overcome, as Emmeline's mother often warned her.

Emmeline, however, was one of those rare members of Society whom everyone liked. So when Sir William asked her for a second dance, and that dance happened to be another waltz, Emmeline followed her heart and accepted. Aunt Patricia was aghast, but she was on the other side of the ballroom and didn't realize what had occurred until one of the tabbies, purring contentedly, whispered in her ear.

To her credit, Aunt Patricia made light of the situation, but she was shocked that her daughter could be so heedless of the rules; one simply didn't dance two waltzes with a man unless he were a husband or fiancé. So she watched helplessly as Emmeline smiled and tripped along in Sir William's arms.

"Fine-looking young lady, your Emmeline," said the dowager countess, joining her.

"Thank you, my lady," murmured Mrs. Kelsey.

"I haven't seen the waltz performed as elegantly," said the dowager. "Living in the country, I have heard of it, but it seemed such a havey-cavey manner of dancing, I dismissed it. Now, however, I can see the advantage of it. I wouldn't have minded such a dance when I was young."

Mrs. Kelsey shook her head and said quietly, "But one shouldn't dance it twice with the same gentleman."

"Why not? Oh, I know all about the rules, but they were meant to be broken. And when one is in love. . . ."

Mrs. Kelsey raised her brows, her eyes following her daughter's progress around the floor. Nodding, she smiled.

"I suppose you are right, my lady."

"I usually am. For instance, I notice that my grandson and your niece are not very intimate." She acknowledged the younger woman's startled glance and explained, "They haven't spent much time together. That's as plain as a pikestaff. I was afraid of that. Charles hasn't allowed anyone to be close to him, except perhaps William, since his parents and brother died when he was eight. I worried about him so. He, of course, thought I was much too interfering." The gray-haired woman gave a throaty laugh

"He's right, too. But the stakes are too high this time; I intend to see to it that he and your Audrey spend all the time it takes to make them fall in love."

"You are very unconventional, my lady. Having arranged the marriage, I assumed you would not believe in marrying for love."

"And you are surprised."

"A little," replied Mrs. Kelsey.

"I thought my husband hung the moon, Mrs. Kelsey. From the first day I set eyes on him, I vowed to wed him. It took him longer, but he became just as devoted to me. I want Charles to have that, too. He's had enough sadness in his life."

"And the arranged marriage?"

"Oh, it wasn't really arranged. We just decided to tell them it was; if either of them had cried off, had found someone else, we wouldn't have stood in the way," said the dowager.

Aunt Patricia smiled. "You have no idea how pleased I am to hear that. I thought Audrey's father was the most selfish man in all of England, wasting her dowry so she would be forced to wed."

The dowager cackled, rubbing her hands together. "That went rather well, but Langston told me it was the only way to set things in motion. Worked, too. Now I just have to push them a little closer to the edge. Just look at him," she said.

Charles tapped his foot impatiently as he watched the dancers. His eyes occasionally sought out Audrey as she was partnered by some other gentleman, but this was not the source of his impatience.

"Calm down, Charles; it's only the boulanger," said William, appearing at his friend's side.

"What?"

"Just mentioning that you cannot call out every man who partners your fiancée in a dance."

"Never intended to. Wasn't even thinking of that," said Charles, never turning his head.

"Did you see Parnell and his family leave?" asked Charles. William nodded, and the earl added, "Sixteen, sixteen people in the private dining room. I shouldn't even be here."

William cleared his throat and took a step back to reveal Emmeline at his elbow.

"What? Are you having a dinner at your house tonight, my lord?" she asked, her brow furrowed.

"No, no, just thinking how lucky Parnell is to get away and have some real refreshments. You know what they serve here," said Charles quickly.

"True, even the drinks are insipid. I do hear that the dinners at that new restaurant called Chez Canard are ever so delicious," said Emmeline. "Perhaps I can persuade Papa and Mama to arrange a supper there after the theater next week."

"A splendid idea, my dear," said William, grinning at his friend.

"Or perhaps a picnic on Friday, if the weather is fine. I understand the restaurant caters, also," said Charles, thinking privately that the last thing he wanted was to go to Chez Canard with his fiancée and sharp-eyed grandmother.

"What a delightful notion," agreed Emmeline.

The boulanger ended, and Charles met Audrey as she was returned to her aunt's side. His grandmother watched them closely.

"I know it is not terribly late," said Charles, "but

I am afraid my grandmother is weary, and I think I should take her home."

"Of course," said Audrey. "How silly of us to stay this long when she has only just arrived today and must be longing for her bed. I apologize, my lady."

"Humph! I can last twice as long as you young people," she asserted. Then her face fell slightly. "But I suppose this is all the excitement we shall have tonight. We might as well go home."

Everyone in their party acquiesced, and they called for the carriages. When they arrived at the Kelsey town house, Aunt Patricia invited them in for tea, but Charles declined before his grandmother could accept. He saw Audrey to the door and bid her a quick farewell. Will announced that he would walk home from the Kelsey town house, so only Charles and the dowager were in the carriage as they made the short journey to Grosvenor Square.

When they entered the hall, the dowager asked him to join her in the library. Charles grumbled, but he followed her.

"Would you like a sherry?" he asked, going to the sideboard and pouring a large measure of brandy for himself.

"Make it brandy," she said.

With a smile of admiration, he poured her a glass and then joined her on the sofa by the fireplace.

"Shall I have someone in to make up a fire?"

"This won't take that long," she said, sipping the strong liquid. Over the rim of her glass, she said abruptly, "You don't love her, do you?"

"Grandmother, I don't intend to discuss my love life with you," Charles said politely.

"What love life? I haven't seen anything in your behavior that remotely resembles a lover's."

"Grandmother," he growled in warning.

She set the glass on the table and leaned toward him, her blue eyes clouded by concern. "You don't have to marry the girl, Charles. All we ever wanted was for our children to be happy. If she can't make you happy, then cry off."

"Grandmother, don't concern yourself with this. Audrey will make me a very good wife. She is reserved, elegant, and beautiful. She will be an excellent hostess . . ." He paused, surprised when she rose and walked away. He waited, wondering what monstrously personal comment she would make next.

When the countess turned, tears were in her eyes. She shook her head and dashed them away angrily. "Have you any idea how that description chills my heart?"

"But it is what you wanted!"

"No! I wanted you to find love. Yes, we arranged the marriage, but there is nothing in writing, nothing binding the two of you together! When I saw Audrey, she was only a child, but she was already strong and independent. I knew she would be perfect for you, for the man you would one day become. At least, the man I hoped you would become."

"I don't understand," he said simply.

"Your father married for money, for property."

"As you want me to do. Isn't that why you chose

Miss Langston? Because her family's property marches with mine?"

"That was secondary. It should have been for your father, too, but all he ever really cared about was money."

"And you did not? Then why did you move to New-market when my parents were killed in that carriage accident?"

"It was your home," she said, joining him once again on the sofa. "You had lost enough; I couldn't make you leave your home. You had always hated visiting us at Drake's Manor."

"True, but why arrange a marriage at all?"

"I was afraid you would be like your father. When you went away to school and were so daring . . . How many times were you sent down? Five? Six?"

"Never mind that now."

"Well, it showed me how wild you were. And then the gambling debts! It was just like your father. I pictured you coming to London, hanging out for a rich wife—any rich wife."

"I never knew," said Charles.

"I tried to keep it from you. Your mother was a sweet woman, but she only tolerated your father. Your father, my son, took advantage of her sweet nature. He was not a very good husband; I think he always resented the fact that he had married her for her money."

"So you tried to make sure I would not make the same mistake."

"Yes, but I have watched you and Miss Langston.

Perhaps she is too cold for you. And you are too cold for her."

Charles smiled, his blue eyes twinkling as he recalled the trembling kiss Audrey had allowed him when he had given her the necklace. Perhaps he had imagined it, but he had sensed a passion beneath that cool exterior. Perhaps he should delve deeper.

He took his grandmother's hands in his and lifted them to his lips, kissing each in turn.

"You must not despair yet, Grandmother. Perhaps Audrey and I do not move at the same speed as you and grandfather did, but give us time. I think we will come to an understanding. I think very highly of Audrey; perhaps it is not love yet, but I find her fascinating. So give us time," he said again.

"I shall try, my dear boy, but patience has never been a virtue with which I have had a close acquaintanceship," admitted the sharp-witted dowager.

"Really? I had no idea," murmured Charles, laughing when she rapped his arm with her fan.

Seven

His grandmother safely stowed in her apartments, Charles changed hurriedly into his "work clothes" and slipped out of the house. Handie, the cabbie, was waiting by the stable gates, as instructed.

"Thought you might o' decided t' call it an early night, sir."

"I probably should have, but I wanted to see that things are going well at the restaurant. We are expecting a large group late tonight."

"Well, I'll have you there in a trice, sir," said the cabbie, carefully not using the earl's title.

At the restaurant, Charles made a quick turn around the room, checking on each cook's work. Then he rolled up his sleeves and began mixing the sugar, heavy cream, and raisin wine for a whipped syllabub which would be mounded on top of the strawberry trifle, a dish of layered sponge cake and custard. It was considered one of the signature dishes of Chez Canard and had to be ordered specially, the day before one came to dine, since it required several stages of preparation. This evening, the dish was to go to the private dining room where Parnell was entertaining his family.

In the dining room, Colette Rimbeau glided between the tables, pausing here and there for a word with one of the customers. The comments she overheard were, as usual, complimentary. If she had heard anything different, she would have immediately corrected the situation, replacing any dissatisfactory dish with another, one more to the diner's liking. This had occurred seldom; Chez Canard had become synonymous with the finest in cuisine and service, and Colette was very proud of "her" restaurant.

This evening, however, she was distracted. Middlehurst's news had taken her by surprise, at a time when she had not yet decided if there was a place for him in her future or not. Now the decision was forced upon her.

Colette Rimbeau was a proud young woman, proud of her French heritage and proud of her resourcefulness. All she had ever desired was what she had, except that the restaurant should belong to her and her father. He had endured much in his life; the younger son of a younger son, her father had received none of the benefits of his noble family, but he had suffered equally, simply because of his name.

When "Mr. Brown" had proposed this enterprise, Colette had seen it as a stepping stone. All she had ever wanted was to own an elegant restaurant; she knew the rich often tired of their hobbies and had hoped, at first, that the earl would also, that he would step aside, allowing her father to purchase the restaurant.

But the earl had proven himself different from other men she had known. He stood shoulder to shoulder with her father, working side by side. The men who frequented her father's tiny inn had either thought her to be there for the taking or had dismissed her completely. Middlehurst, however, respected her and her opinions. She, in turn, had come to respect him, as a chef and a man.

And lately, she had actually grown fond of the earl, fond enough to consider, in the distant future, another possibility—marriage to him. She knew such an alliance would be unthinkable to most members of the Ton, but the earl, as she knew, was not like others.

There was no question of love; to Colette, it was a question of ambition. If marriage to the earl—or to anyone, for that matter—would help her attain her goal, then she could see no fault in it. And she never doubted her ability to win him away from this insipid English lady.

Colette entered the kitchens, her dark eyes immediately seeking the earl. He was busy stirring some sauce, his attention diverted. Normally, his eyes followed her whenever she entered the kitchen. Suddenly, he looked up and smiled.

Colette's eyes dropped; she didn't want him to read the uncertainty in them. What would happen when he married? She knew enough about the gentry to realize this new wife would never countenance his cooking in the restaurant. She would probably insist that he sell to the highest bidder, and that would be the end of it, the end of her reign over Chez Canard, the end of all her hopes.

Yes, thought Colette, the matter is urgent. If I want things to continue as they are, I will have to be bold.

"Tu rêves tout éveillée, ma petite," said Rimbeau.

Colette blushed and turned away. "No, Papa, I am not daydreaming. I am devising a plan."

"A plan? For what?"

"For us, Papa, for us. Excuse me, I must return to the dining room."

As she left the kitchens, she ran into Mr. Parnell, tipsy from too much champagne and bent on congratulating the chef on the excellent repast he and his family had enjoyed.

"I am sorry, monsieur, but no one is allowed to pass this way except the waiters," said Colette, carefully blocking his passage.

"You're a pretty little thing," he said, his eyes taking on an owlish appearance as he tried to focus on her. "Very pretty. I tell you what, pretty one, I'll buy you a new bonnet if you'll just let me by."

"I am sorry, monsieur. That is not possible," she said, shifting to the other side of the corridor as he tried to slip by her.

"Here now, you're making me dizzy, girl."

"Then you should go and sit down."

"Don't want to. Want to . . . Oh, I forget," said Parnell, holding his head.

"Come along, Monsieur Parnell. I will take you back to the dining room."

"What? Oh, thank you, miss. You are most kind,"

he mumbled, leaning heavily on her as he returned to the private parlour.

When Colette returned to the kitchens, Charles approached her, bowing over her hand. "You are a marvel, Colette Rimbeau. I don't know what I should do without you."

Colette blushed prettily and, with a saucy wink, said boldly, "Or I you, Mr. Brown."

Audrey woke in the early afternoon the next day, her eyes red and puffy from lack of sleep. Her maid had entered the room twice, each time bringing fresh coffee to tempt her mistress awake, but the ploy had failed.

Dragging herself out of bed, Audrey stretched her stiff muscles. She allowed Millie to dress her in a soft yellow morning gown before she settled on the dark blue fainting couch, her coffee beside her and a novel in her lap. Reading, however, was not as enthralling as her memories, and the novel lay neglected.

Her thoughts drifted bask to Almack's and the dances she and Charles had shared. But even now, in the light of day, these thoughts did not comfort her. Instead, once again, she relived each word, each gesture. And just like the night before, doubts about this man she was to wed came creeping out of their dark holes to plague her.

Charles acted as if he enjoyed her company, but there was nothing of the lover in his manner. He held her just as he ought during their waltzes. Why, then, did she somehow feel shortchanged?

She recalled the way Emmeline gazed up at Sir William; he, too, had appeared oblivious of everyone and everything but her when they danced. And when they were dancing with others, William's eyes often strayed to Emmeline. Audrey tried to tell herself that Charles was doubtlessly watching her in the same possessive manner when she was not looking, but she knew he was not. She would have felt his eyes on her.

No, Charles had been the perfect gentleman, dancing with a variety of young ladies, even waltzing with one dark haired beauty—the granddaughter of a friend of his grandmother. Yes, her fiancé was a perfect gentleman. Drat the man!

Such chilling thoughts crawled out of bed with her on that dreary Thursday morning and would not give her peace. Audrey knew she was expecting too much of him. He liked her; he might even admire her, but he didn't love her—not the way she loved him. The realization threatened to weigh her down, to crush her heart.

There was a quiet knock on the door.

"Enter," she said wearily.

Beamish opened the door and stepped inside, pushing it closed behind him. "I beg your pardon for intruding, miss, but there is a person asking to see you."

"What sort of person, Beamish?"

"A foreign lady. At least, I think she is a lady, but it is difficult to say."

"What nationality is she?"

"At first I thought she was English, but then I detected a slight accent. French, I think."

"And she wants to see me?"

"Yes, she was quite specific, miss. I put her in the ladies' morning room. If you wish, I will send her about her business."

"No, no," said Audrey, curiosity animating her face. "Just stay close by, please."

"Of course, miss," said the butler, standing aside for her to pass.

Audrey opened the door cautiously, her instincts warning of some ominous incident about to take place. At first she thought the room was empty. Then there was a movement near the fireplace, and a figure rose from the delicate chair. Taking a deep breath, Audrey moved forward, hand outstretched.

"How do you do, Miss . . . ?"

"My name is not important," said the figure, ignoring the gesture of welcome. She moved slightly, bringing her face into the light.

Audrey let her hand fall. "What may I do for you?" she asked, her tone impersonal and cold.

"Nothing. I merely wanted to meet the woman who is to wed Lord Middlehurst."

"Are you acquainted with my fiancé?" asked Audrey, her manner growing more formal by the moment. Who do you think you are? she wanted to demand, but good manners directed her actions and her words.

"You are very beautiful, Miss Langston, but I think perhaps the earl needs more than a frosted beauty."

"I don't recall his mentioning you," said Audrey.

"And I really have nothing to say to you since you will not give me your name."

"I am Colette, just Colette."

"His mistress?"

Now it was her visitor's turn to stiffen with anger.

"I am no man's mistress. No, I am merely interested in the earl."

Audrey turned on her heel and marched to the door. Opening it, she said dismissively, "Odd, he has never mentioned having any interest in a woman named Colette. Beamish will show you to the door."

"I will go, Miss Langston, but I should warn you. There are things you don't know about your fiancé—things that will not please you."

"I have no intention of discussing my fiancé with you," said Audrey.

Colette shrugged her slender shoulders and said, "It doesn't matter. I have decided to have the Earl of Middlehurst myself."

With a grand air, she swept past Audrey. Beamish, waiting beside the morning room, escorted their visitor to the front door.

The butler returned quickly to Audrey's side, a glass in his hand. "Come sit down and drink this, miss," he said, guiding her back into the room and settling her on the settee. She took a tiny sip and thrust the glass away, but he insisted. "You've had a shock, miss. This will help."

"Who was she, Beamish? Did she give you her card?"

The butler nodded, fumbling in his pocket for a battered calling card. "She handed this to me as she left; she said she thought you might like to come and dine some evening. I assured her you would not,"

Audrey read the card and frowned. "Now why would a woman who works at Chez Canard call on me?" she wondered out loud. Privately, she had a thousand questions, but she didn't voice these to the butler.

Beamish shook his head, saying, "I have no idea, miss. I wouldn't worry about it. And you can be certain I shan't allow a pretty face to wrangle her way into the house again!"

Audrey smiled. "You allowed yourself to be wrangled, Beamish?"

"It shan't happen again, miss," said the butler, his dignity sadly bent.

"No, you did the right thing. It is just that there is some mystery afoot, and I intend to get to the bottom of it. You must tell no one about this visitor, Beamish."

"But your aunt. . . ."

"Is better off not knowing. I will be careful," she promised, downing the remainder of the glass in one gulp. The liquid burned her throat, but she felt suddenly equal to anything.

"Have the carriage brought around, Beamish. Millie and I have a call to make."

"Very good, miss."

Audrey shifted uncomfortably on the velvet seat of the carriage. She had been sitting thus for an hour and had long since given up any claim to sanity. She

was waiting and watching, outside the restaurant
Chez Canard, because of a peculiar visitor named
Colette. She didn't know for whom or what she
waited.

Not for the first time, Cal leaned down to say, "Th'
horses, miss, the horses."

"Just another minute or two," she replied again.

"But, miss . . . Carriage coming, miss," he whispered.

Audrey chuckled quietly. Her mysterious mission
had evidently caught hold of Cal's imagination, too.
Millie, asleep on the facing seat, was the only occu-
pant of the carriage oblivious of the momentous
event about to occur.

"Just some chap in a hansom cab, miss," said Cal,
obviously disappointed.

But Audrey sat forward, watching the man, dressed
in a rough coat, descend from the carriage and flip
a coin to the driver. There was something about those
slender hands, the long fingers. He pulled his hat
down on his head and slipped through the side door
of the restaurant. Audrey sat back against the velvet
cushions; a long breath, almost a whistle, escaped
through her teeth.

Charles!

Her eyes caught a movement above the door. In
the upstairs window, a curtain moved, and Audrey
found herself gazing into the eyes of the young
woman named Colette. With a smug smile and a nod,
her mysterious visitor let the curtain fall.

Audrey tapped the root. "Let's go home, Cal," she
said glumly.

As the carriage pulled away, Millie woke and sat up. "I'm so sorry I fell asleep, miss. Did I miss anything?"

"No, nothing," Audrey said quickly, wondering how she could mask her heartbreak so easily.

When Audrey arrived home, Beamish stopped her in the hall, his curiosity making him lose his professional manner long enough to inquire, "Did you discover who she was, miss?"

"Not precisely, but it doesn't matter. Is my aunt at home?" asked Audrey, wanting some distraction to help her forget what she had learned.

She could think of no logical reason for Charles to be entering the side door of the restaurant except an illicit tryst. The woman lived abovestairs; she had lied when she'd said she wasn't his mistress.

"No, miss, she and Miss Riggs are making calls. Miss Emmeline and her maid are in the salon with Sir William."

"Thank you, Beamish. And thank you for keeping my confidences," she added.

"It is a privilege, miss," said the old man with a bow.

Audrey started slowly up the stairs; then she paused, the seed of an idea beginning to germinate in her head. She retraced her steps and entered the drawing room, sending Emmeline's maid away with a cheery, "You can go about your business, Mary. I shall stay and visit with your mistress and Sir William."

The maid bobbed a curtsey and disappeared.

Sir William started to rise, but Audrey waved him

back into the chair beside the window. Emmeline's head was lowered as she studied the backgammon board.

"Hello, Sir William," said Audrey quietly, for she knew her cousin took her games seriously. "When you are finished, I would like to have a word with you."

"Certainly, Miss Langston," said William, his whisper clearly audible. "Your cousin is just realizing she cannot possibly win, and she cannot believe I have so soundly defeated her."

Smiling, Emmeline pushed away from table and said roundly, "He cheats!"

"I do not!" he replied cheerily, his green eyes twinkling. "Besides, it isn't necessary to cheat when one's opponent is so singularly lacking in ability."

Audrey waited for Emmeline's explosion of indignation. She, who competed in everything, would surely not tolerate such a slur!

But Emmeline amazed her cousin by giggling in the most feminine manner and declaring, "I allowed you to win!"

"You did not!" he returned. "And now you must pay the forfeit! Your cousin is witness to your defeat."

"And what is the forfeit?" asked Emmeline coyly.

"I haven't decided. A lock of hair, perhaps? No! I have it! The next time we race in the park, you will give me a head start!"

The laughing couple turned to include Audrey in their nonsensical exchange. When they saw her pale blue eyes were swimming with tears, their manners changed abruptly, and they rushed to her, leading her to the sofa and sitting on either side, patting her hands ineffectually.

Audrey's bout of self-pity was short-lived, and she was soon pouring out the tale of her strange visitor and the ill-fated afternoon. When she had finished, she wiped away her tears and accepted Sir William's handkerchief to blow her nose.

"The cad," said Emmeline. "And what nerve she had! Well, William, have you nothing to say? Did you know about this woman?"

Audrey wondered fleetingly when Emmeline had dropped his title. William, who had moved away to stare out the window, turned to them, his face in shadow so she couldn't read his expression. His red hair glinted with gold as the afternoon sun shone through it, creating a fiery halo.

"Well?" demanded Emmeline impatiently.

"Leave us for a moment, Emmeline," said William.

"I will not! If there is some mystery here, you are not going to keep me out of it! Besides, it isn't proper to leave the two of you alone!"

"Very well, you may be of some help to your cousin," he said, rejoining them.

He took the delicate chair across from the sofa, drawing it closer and looking around to be certain they were alone. With a shiver, each young lady leaned forward.

"This is not my secret to tell, but I can see that your mind has raced in every direction except the correct one. Charles is not meeting this Colette for . . . That is, she is not and has never been his mistress. I see you don't believe me, but you must. I'm telling you the truth."

"Then why would he arrive at this restaurant in an unmarked hansom cab? He has a perfectly good carriage—several, in fact."

"Exactly, but as you said, the cab is unmarked. His carriage has his crest on it, and secrecy is of the utmost importance."

Audrey's shoulders slumped in defeat, but Emmeline demanded, "Never mind that. Why was this person waiting for him upstairs?"

"She lives upstairs with her father. Charles doesn't go to Chez Canard to see her; he goes there to cook," said William, running a hand through his short curls. "And I am sworn to secrecy, but dash it all, I couldn't let you think he. . . ."

Frowning, Emmeline declared, "What nonsense!"

"Cooking?" said Audrey. "You want me to believe that Charles, a peer of the realm, is a cook at that restaurant?"

William nodded, saying uncomfortably, "I daresay he would prefer the term chef."

"But why would he do such a thing? Surely he has enough funds—"

"Charles doesn't do it for the money. And he's not just a chef, he is *the* chef. He owns Chez Canard."

"William, this is the most bizarre story I have ever heard. I know you are trying to protect Audrey, but you should tell her the truth," said Emmeline.

"I promise you, I am telling the truth. Even the name was his idea. Think about it. Charles *Drake*—a

male duck—and *canard* is French for duck," said Sir
William as if this closed the matter.

"But why?" asked Audrey, feeling the stone in the
pit of her stomach starting to dissolve.

"Charles finds it amusing, and then there is the
matter of a little wager, which I shall now have to pay
since I have given the game away," he grumbled.

"But why a restaurant?" Emmeline wanted to
know.

"Charles was the best chef on the Peninsula. When
we were bivouacked in some godforsaken hole, he
managed to make even the poorest meal palatable.
When we returned home, he was fine for a while.
Then the old boredom began last fall, and he decided to open Chez Canard. I told him he was crazy.
'Can you imagine what the Ton will say of this?' I
asked. But Charles is like a horse with the bit between
its teeth; nothing will stop him."

"But isn't Chez Canard the place everyone is talking about?" said Audrey. "Why, he even mentioned
having them cater a picnic next week."

"Yes," William replied. "You have to give the old
boy that. He has made a success of the venture."

"That still does not explain this Colette," said Emmeline. "He must have encouraged her for her to
come here this morning."

"I don't think so, but I can't say for certain. She is
a very calculating female. I don't think she would
give any man the time of day unless he could benefit
her in some way," said William, reflecting on the set-
down Colette had given him. He looked up to Em-

meline's shrewd scrutiny and tugged at his cravat which had suddenly become too tight.

"Are you going to confront Charles about the restaurant?" he asked Audrey anxiously.

"No, I don't care about the restaurant, and I wouldn't wish to betray your confidences, Sir William," said Audrey.

"But Aude, if you made him give up the restaurant, this Colette wouldn't have the opportunity to . . . well, you know," said Emmeline.

"True, but I would be left to always wonder if he preferred her to me, if he regretted marrying me," said Audrey, nervously knotting and unknotting Sir William's white handkerchief. Then she rose.

"I say, Miss Langston, Audrey, you don't mean to confront Charles, do you? I mean, if you decide to do so, I hope you will warn me first."

"No, I don't think I shall let Charles know I am aware of his little secret."

"But what are you going to do, Audrey?" asked Emmeline, watching as her cousin crossed the room, and sat down at the delicate escritoire in the corner.

"I am sending a note to Madame Dufour, asking her to come tomorrow morning at ten o'clock with new pattern books and fabric swatches."

"Whatever for?" asked Emmeline.

Audrey sealed the short missive and rang for a footman. When he had received his instructions and departed, she turned back to the couple on the sofa.

"If this Colette female is as calculating as you think, Sir William, then I have my work cut out for me. Earlier, I was ready to beg off the betrothal, but now . . . I think I would very much like to see this Colette creature lose this game, and I must fight in every way I know how."

Emmeline chuckled, but William still looked puzzled.

"And Madame Dufour?" he asked.

"New gowns, William. There is nothing better for a woman preparing to wage a battle," said Emmeline. To Audrey, she added, "New, *daring* gowns!"

Charles, unaware of the plots whirring around him, spent a pleasant afternoon and early evening in the kitchen at the restaurant. His grandmother had informed him that she would remain at home that night, in her private sitting room, catching up on correspondence. Dismissed from dancing attendance on her, he was free to stay as long as he wished at the restaurant. Later he planned to look in on his club and play a few hands of cards.

"Mr. Brown," said Colette, sidling up to him. "I need to speak to you about the accounts, if I may."

"Is there some problem?" he asked casually, knowing that Colette's efficiency would not allow a very large problem to arise.

"A small one, but I would like your advice, sir."

With that, she turned and glided into his office. He followed, watching her graceful movements as she sat down behind the large desk. He closed the door.

"Here, this letter arrived this morning, saying we have not paid this bill. I know that I have, but the tradesman does not like to deal with females, and he refuses to believe me. As you can see from this entry, that account was paid."

Instead of pushing the ledger toward him, she merely pointed to the column of figures. To get a better look, Charles was forced to circle the desk and lean over her shoulder. Her perfume filled his nostrils.

"See?"

"Um, yes. Well, perhaps I can have a word with the fellow," said Charles.

Twisting slightly and cutting her eyes at him, she whispered, "Thank you, my lord. That would be most helpful."

Charles straightened, clearing his throat. This is wrong, his mind screamed, but he was not thinking with his mind at that moment. He merely sensed that he must get out of the office and away from Colette, the siren.

"Well, I shall certainly take care of that tomorrow, my . . . Colette. For now, I have an engagement, and I really should be going." Charles made good his escape, hurrying toward the cab like a man in the desert who spies an oasis.

"Good evenin', sir. Goin' 'ome a little early t'night, aren't ye?"

"A little, Handie, just a little."

"I understand you're goin' to wed Miss Langston. I hear nice things about that one. She's a real lady."

"Yes, a real lady," said Charles.

He berated himself all the way home. He told himself Colette had no reason to act as she had; he certainly hadn't led her to believe . . . But Charles was an honest man, and though he hated to admit it, he knew the looks they sometimes exchanged might easily be construed as flirting.

Still, she knew he was betrothed. Why would she suddenly try to entice him into a situation where he might lose his head? And how would she have reacted if he had kissed her? They had been so close, he could easily . . .

This thought was replaced by the image of Audrey as they waltzed the night before at Almack's, her silver-blond hair so close he could have kissed it, her eyes shining as she peered up at him, laughing at some witticism.

Perhaps she was not as passionate as Colette seemed to be. Still, Audrey was well bred with manners to match. He was fortunate that she had agreed to wed him, yet he had taken their betrothal and her for granted.

"You stupid fool," he growled.

"Beg pardon, sir," said the driver.

"Nothing, Handie, nothing."

When Charles reached his room, he tore off the old clothes, ringing for his valet and shouting for hot water. He strode over to the small desk on which a stack of invitations lay, and he scattered them, sorting through the stiff, white cards until he spied the ones for that evening. He had refused both the musicale and Lady Wentworth's ball, but he knew they would welcome him anyway, and he felt sure he would find Audrey at one place or the other.

"Dancing shoes," he snapped when his valet entered the room. Thirty minutes later, he added the final touch as he placed the pin in the folds of his cravat, its sapphire encircled by diamonds to match the pendant he had given Audrey.

"If Sir William should happen to call, tell him I have gone to Lady Wentworth's ball," said Charles, hurrying out the door.

Lady Wentworth was another eccentric of the Ton. She never wore dresses, always trousers, fashioned after the costumes found in a sheik's harem. Her husband, long inured to this oddity, had taken to wearing his long dressing gown any time they entertained at home. Still, though their appearances were fantastic, their entertainments were extremely proper and ordinary, almost to the point of being dull.

When the Wentworths greeted Audrey, Lady Wentworth eyed her new gown with her lorgnette and said shrewdly, "Now that's bound to attract the gentlemen, my dear."

"Thank you, my lady," Audrey replied, tugging Emmeline away quickly.

Riggs, hurrying to catch them up, commented, "I told you everyone would remark upon that gown."

"Oh, do not tease Audrey so, Riggs," protested Emmeline. "Perhaps the royal blue is a bit bold—"

"It is not the color," said Riggs, eyeing the low décolletage with one raised brow.

Audrey surveyed the assembled guests, knowing

Charles had declared he would not attend, but hoping that perhaps he had changed his mind. But he had not, and only Sir William and Lord Asherton crossed the room to join them.

"I might as well have waited until tomorrow for Madame Dufour to come to the house," said Audrey.

"Nonsense, then you would not have known about this gown which she just happened to have on hand, finished and unclaimed. You look very fine in it!" said Emmeline loyally.

"I look half-naked in it," whispered Audrey before turning to greet the two gentlemen.

Judging from the way Lord Asherton's eyes kept straying to her bosom, she knew her assessment was right. Riggs, as blunt as ever, had declared the royal blue gown fit only for a lightskirt. She had probably been correct.

But as the evening progressed, even Riggs had to admit, Audrey was very much the belle of the ball. She never lacked for a partner; it seemed the gentlemen were seeing the proper Miss Langston in a different light.

Audrey, declining all offers of a quadrille after five sets so she could rest, sat down beside Riggs and whispered, "I suppose you are right, Riggs. This gown is much too bold."

"Not really, Audrey." Riggs shook her head, unwilling to have one of "her girls" disparage herself. "I have been looking at the other gowns. Just look at Lady Goforth; her gown pushes her breasts up so that they almost touch her chin. And that young lady over there; hers is positively indecent. Your gown is most

suitable in comparison. And you are, after all, a betrothed lady, not in your first Season. No, I think you
look very well."

"I couldn't agree more," said Charles, surprising
both ladies by his sudden appearance behind their
chairs. "And I hope you have saved at least one dance
for me."

"Charles! I didn't think you were coming tonight,"
said Audrey, her eyes alight with pleasure.

"No more did I, but I asked myself which I would
really prefer, being in your delightful company or
winning a fortune at the turn of a card. You, of
course, won out handily."

"Why, I believe you are being gallant," said Audrey.

"I can but try," he said, looking up to glare at a
young man with coal black hair and a puce coat.

But the young man was proof against the earl's
glare and, with only a slight squeak in his voice, said,
"I believe this is my dance, Miss Langston."

"Yes, of course, Mr. Pennington."

Charles watched as the couple took the floor; he
cursed under his breath when he realized it was the
waltz. He should have turned the impudent whelp
away! The tall, impudent whelp, he added, raising
one brow and glowering as he realized the young
man's height gave him an excellent vantage point
from which to gawk at Audrey's breasts. Yet he had
allowed him to lead her away! He might as well have
stabbed himself in the back!

"Doesn't she look lovely in that color," said Riggs,
twisting the knife in further.

"Yes, Miss Riggs, lovely."

Charles spent the next hour watching Audrey dance with first one and then another. When he suggested she might want to turn them away in favor of a dance with her fiancé, she opened those blue eyes as wide as she could and demurred, explaining that she didn't wish to be unkind.

Finally, the strains of a waltz were struck up again. Charles, flexing his stiff muscles as he pushed away from the column he had been supporting, stepped between his friend Asherton and Audrey.

"You'll give up your place for me, won't you, Asherton?" he said, clenching his fists.

"What? Oh, certainly, if Miss Langston doesn't mind."

Charles glared at Asherton, and he added hastily, "That is, of course she won't mind. Much rather dance with you, Middlehurst, I'll be bound."

"Thank you, Lord Asherton," said Audrey, hiding her mirth behind wide eyes.

"Impertinent popinjay," muttered Charles, leading Audrey to the floor.

"I think Lord Asherton is a very considerate gentleman," said Audrey.

"I daresay you do," grumbled Charles, taking her in his arms. "You probably think all the gentlemen who have been clamoring for the opportunity to ogle you tonight are very considerate."

"That is insulting, my lord, both to me and the gentlemen who have been so kind as to ask me for a dance, especially when you were not here earlier," said Audrey.

"And how many of them have danced with you before?" he asked coldly.

"You, sir, are being boorish."

"And you, madam, are being foolish. While I grant that you are very beautiful at any given time, the men who have been so eager to stand up with you tonight are not doing so for the beauty of your face."

"Oh!"

"I daresay they haven't so much as glanced at that pretty face of yours!"

Audrey tried to pull out of his arms, but he refused to release her.

Pursing her lips, she stared just past his ear and refused to speak to him for the remainder of the dance, which suited the fuming earl just fine. When the music stopped, Charles bowed briefly over her hand and walked away. Audrey glanced around, wondering how many people had noticed, but everyone appeared to be too busy going into the dining room for the supper buffet. With Charles gone, she would have no one to partner her.

"Riggs," she said, spying the older woman in the crowd. Riggs abandoned her friends and joined Audrey.

"What is it, my dear girl?"

Audrey, near tears, shook her head. "I am going to have the carriage brought around. I have the headache and want to go home. I'll send it back for you and Emmeline."

"Nonsense, child, we will all go home."

"No, no, I don't need any company, and Emmeline

is enjoying herself so. Please, I'll be fine. Good night."

Audrey tapped her foot impatiently as she waited for the carriage. Biting the inside of her jaw, she managed not to break down. But once she was in the carriage, she could no longer withstand her emotions, and the sobs that had threatened for so long, broke loose.

She managed to regain her composure before the footman opened the door and let down the steps. Keeping her head down, she entered the house, explaining briefly to Beamish that he should send the carriage back for Riggs and Emmeline.

Once inside her room, Audrey allowed Millie to dress her for bed. Then she waited for the tears to start again. But they refused to come, refused to give her that release.

Instead, her mind raced, first with anger, then indignation, and then finally with amusement.

She blew out the candles and pulled the counterpane up under her chin. In the darkness, she smiled.

"Well, Audrey my girl, you have been wanting some kind of reaction from Charles. I would say you got one tonight!"

Eight

Charles did not call on Friday or Saturday. Audrey tried to keep her spirits high, but it was difficult. She kept her appointment with Madame Dufour and ordered four new gowns and a riding habit. The pearl gray habit was fitted like a man's coat, except that the neckline was cleverly cut to reveal a generous expanse of neck. It was not risqué, but it gave the illusion of being so. The gowns were not quite as daring as the royal blue; nevertheless, Emmeline christened them Audrey's courtesan gowns, sending both girls into gales of laughter while Riggs shook her head and regally looked down her nose at them both.

Audrey spied Charles at St. Paul's church on Sunday for services. He avoided her eyes during worship, but outside, afterward, his grandmother made certain the two families met for a chat.

"How are you, my dear child?" asked the dowager, pulling Audrey to one side.

"I am fine, my lady. And you?"

"I really should not complain, but Charles is so very dull. I never realized how boring he had be-

come. You and your charming cousin must come for
a visit this afternoon."

"Why, thank you, but—"

"Oh, do say you will come. Charles will disappear
as he always does, leaving me alone for hours on
end," said the dowager, her voice plaintive.

Audrey felt sure she knew how her elusive fiancé
was passing the time, and decided she might need to
enlist the dowager countess's help. She smiled and
accepted the invitation. Charles glanced at her then,
but she couldn't read his expression.

"At what time, my lady?"

"Shall we say five o'clock."

"Thank you, my lady. I look forward to it."

"Audrey, are you sure you want to wear that particular gown?" asked Emmeline.

"What is the matter with it?"

"Well, nothing, except that it is rather plain."

"You mean ugly," said Audrey.

"Yes, I do. I thought you were trying to attract Lord
Middlehurst, not repel him."

Audrey laughed and straightened the puce-colored
gown, adding a lace fichu to the modest neckline. "If
Charles is there, I count on this to catapult him into
some sort of conversation. It seems the only way to get
a reaction from the man is to do something outrageous."

"That gown is certainly outrageous," said Emmeline.

Audrey studied her image in the cheval glass. "Yes,
it is, but this silence has gone on long enough."

"And if he is not there?"

"Then I don't really care how I look," said Audrey, settling a coal-scuttle bonnet on her silvery curls.

"You have become very peculiar, Audrey. I simply don't understand how you can be so calm about Middlehurst, knowing he is spending almost every waking hour with that woman! If William did that—"

"But Charles is not spending time with her precisely; she just happens to be there, too. Besides, I will get to spend the next two days with him."

"Oh, yes, the Brabingers' breakfast tomorrow. I can't wait. William has promised to show me how to hold a bow and shoot an arrow," said Emmeline with a gurgle of laughter.

"But you already know how," said Audrey. "You can outshoot all four of your brothers."

"Ah, but William doesn't know that. And at the Middlehurst's picnic on Tuesday, he has promised to row me down the river."

"And you didn't bother to tell him that you have the strength of ten men in those dainty little arms, did you?"

"I wouldn't want to spoil the fun." Emmeline laughed.

"Well, just try not to fall in. If he saw you swimming to shore, it would crush all his illusions!" said Audrey.

"I shall be very careful!"

Charles's staff was on alert; the future Countess of Middlehurst was coming for a visit, and everything had to be perfect! Cook spent the afternoon baking;

the maids and footmen spent their time polishing. Charles, lounging in his dressing gown in his sitting room, prepared himself to ignore the entire affair. But when he heard the hubbub of their arrival, he couldn't prevent himself from slipping out to the top of the stairs and sneaking a peek.

A deep rumble of laughter, quickly hushed, escaped his throat when Audrey entered the hall. The sound made her look up, their eyes locking for a second before she and Emmeline followed the butler into the drawing room where his grandmother waited.

Whistling, Charles straightened and returned to his room for his coat. She is full of surprises, he thought as he shrugged into the tight-fitting garment. He checked the mirror, straightening his Belcher neckerchief. He smiled; that alone would cause his grandmother a flash of displeasure. He ran his fingers through his hair, letting it fall where it might. Two could play at this absurd game of fashion roulette.

He knew Audrey; she was always dressed in quiet elegance—except for that blue gown at the Wentworths' ball, of course. Now she was dressed as a dowd, no doubt to teach him a lesson for criticizing her.

"Good afternoon, ladies," he said when he entered the drawing room.

After a sweeping bow, he settled himself in an uncomfortable chair across from Audrey and accepted a cup of tea. Inwardly, he grinned; Audrey was pouring out—his grandmother's suggestion, he felt sure.

He wondered if she had passed inspection. He could have told his grandmother, had she bothered to ask, that Audrey was the epitome of all the feminine arts. Well, arts like pouring out; in the other feminine arts, those which would appeal to him, she had no experience whatsoever.

His grandmother, looking him up and down, declared, "We don't mind waiting while you get dressed properly, Charles."

"I am dressed, Grandmother. Do you mean you don't like my spotted neckcloth? I assure you, it is all the rage."

"You look like a circus performer," she said, frowning fiercely.

"I think it is very fetching," Audrey remarked, smiling.

"I thought you might, my dear," said Charles. "I know I can always count on you to be current on these important issues. You are ever dressed in the first stare of fashion."

"You are too kind, Middlehurst. Do you like this bonnet?" asked Audrey, turning her head this way and that to show each angle of the ugly affair.

"Quite becoming," he said, his eyes laughing with her.

"Must need glasses," muttered Emmeline.

"And the color? I was afraid puce might be a trifle too bold," said Audrey, causing Charles to choke on his tea. "Oh, dear, you will spot your spotted neck cloth!"

Emmeline and the dowager countess looked from

one participant to the other in this mysterious exchange.

Charles cleared his throat and shook his head. "You win, my dear. I can't keep up with you. I was doing fine until that comment about puce being too bold. I cry *pax*. You are too quick for me."

"You are too kind, my lord," said Audrey, bowing her head.

She knew she had won the point, but it had been a near thing. And now what? Would they go back to being the friends they were before the blue dress incident? That was not enough if she were to triumph over Colette.

"Do you go to the Brabingers' breakfast tomorrow?" asked her ladyship.

"Yes, we are looking forward to it. Aren't we, Emmeline?" said Audrey.

"Yes, yes. I shall have to get plenty of rest tonight if I am to last from three o'clock until dawn," her cousin said, dimpling prettily.

"You young people are too soft. In my day, we considered it requisite to dance from dusk to dawn without a single break!"

"But we have never been as young as you, Grandmother," said Charles, winking at Audrey. "I hope each of you will save me some dances."

"Of course, my lord," Emmeline declared.

"And you, my dear? Will you waltz with me?" asked Charles, his manner sobering. And only me, he wanted to add, but he was unsure of her response.

"I would love to, my . . . lord," said Audrey.

* * *

Monday turned out to be a fine day, the weather cooperating fully for the success of the Brabingers' breakfast. Their house was built after the style of an Italian villa with columned terraces that led gradually toward the formal gardens. Beyond these, tents had been erected on the lawn to accommodate the crush of guests.

The Kelsey family, with Audrey and the dowager countess, made the journey in the comfort of the earl's huge traveling carriage. Charles and William rode alongside on horseback. When they arrived, the gentlemen secured a large table in the shade of an old oak tree. The older ladies settled down for a comfortable coze, greeting and commenting on the parade of people passing by.

Audrey, dressed in one of her new gowns, accepted Charles's arm and followed Emmeline and William on a tour of the gardens. Emmeline, who was not a gardener, admired the full, lush blooms, but she was not moved by its beauty. Audrey paused by each blossom, testing its fragrance, pondering on the plant's suitability if it were added to their garden back home.

"Come along, Audrey. William is going to teach me all about archery." Emmeline's her tiny store of patience was exhausted.

"This should be interesting," said Charles. "Will, the last time I saw you with a bow in your hands, you nearly put out your eye. Didn't it take a physician to sew up your cheek?"

"He exaggerates." William scowled at his friend.

"You two run along. Audrey and I will catch up with you," said Charles. When they were alone, he said quietly, "That is a very becoming gown you are wearing."

Audrey smiled at him, recalling their raillery the previous afternoon. Then she plunged into the deep waters, knowing the air had to be cleared between them. "What you are really trying to do is salve your conscience about the other night."

"The other night?" asked Charles, studying the tops of his shoes. With a schoolboy grin, he begged her forgiveness and looked up, saying, "No, I am trying to begin again, forgetting the other night. You were quite properly attired, quite beautifully attired. I was boorish and rude, but I have a simple explanation; I was jealous."

Audrey's breast swelled with gratification.

"That is a new gown, too, is it not?" he asked, his eyes resting briefly on the creamy rise of breasts which then disappeared into the jonquil yellow bodice.

Audrey frowned. This gown was certainly not indecent; it was nothing like the royal blue. It was almost as conservative as her usual style. What was this new obsession Charles had with her gowns? Her satisfaction over his admission of jealousy was diminished. If all he wanted was a possession, then theirs would be a very colorless marriage.

"You are very quiet." He reached out, touching one blond curl that had escaped her bonnet.

"I apologize; I was wool-gathering. Why don't we join Emmeline and Sir William?"

She started forward, leaving the confounded earl to follow. Charles wondered what he had said to discomfit her. He had paid her pretty compliments; he had apologized for his boorish behavior. Nothing I do seems to advance my suit with her, he thought crossly.

When they arrived on the scene, Charles forgot his uncertainty. Before their very eyes, bedlam had broken loose. Taking Audrey's hand, he hurried forward.

Sir William, instead of quietly teaching Emmeline how to shoot the arrow, was standing a few feet away from her, busily writing in his betting book. Masculine and feminine voices mingled, calling out sums of money. Emmeline was calmly testing the strength of her bow.

"All bets done?" asked Sir William.

"What the devil is going on?" demanded Charles.

"Nothing! Emmeline here bet she could hit the bull's-eye two times out of three. Asherton bet she couldn't, and the rest, as they say, is history. All right, my dear, are you ready?"

"Emmeline," said Audrey, "are you sure this is wise?"

"It's all in fun, Aude," the dark-haired girl replied with a mischievous grin. Whispering, she added, "I'm going to make a fortune. Just watch!"

"Emmeline. . . ."

"Move back, Audrey. You can't stop her," said Charles, irritation in his voice.

"Perhaps I don't think I need to," said Audrey, her displeasure with him growing by the moment. "You needn't stay if you are afraid of being associated with us."

"Audrey, I didn't mean that . . . By Jove, she did it! Square in the bull's-eye! She'll never make it again," he added.

"Would you care to place a wager on that, my lord?" said Audrey.

"One hundred pounds?"

"Done!" she replied, crossing her fingers in the folds of her skirt so he would not know how uncertain she was of her cousin's aim.

A groan went up from half the crowd as the next arrow went astray. Emmeline turned and winked at Audrey as she picked up another arrow.

"Last chance!" called out one male voice.

"To win," said Emmeline with a smile.

She pulled back on the string, sighting the target carefully. She released it, and with a whir, it sped toward the bull's-eye, landing neatly in the center.

Huzzahs and groans mingled briefly before everyone, even the losers, cheered for Emmeline.

"Wherever did you learn to shoot a bow like that?" William laughed.

"Never, ever, wager against a girl with four brothers when it comes to the manly arts. I had to learn all of them in order to defend myself," said Emmeline tartly.

"All of them?" teased William.

"Well, some of them," she admitted with a blush.

"I know you are a bruising rider; our races in the park have shown me that. What about fencing?" William asked.

"No, no one would teach me that. I think it was because they are all so very bad at it. Would you teach me?" she asked Sir William sweetly.

"Perhaps I should; at least that would be something I could win with you," he replied.

"For a time," she said, grinning up at him.

Bringing the conversation back to the mundane, Charles said, "So your brothers taught you to shoot a bow and arrow. What of you, Audrey? Did you learn alongside Emmeline?"

"No, I am not so intrepid as my cousin. I do like to ride, but I can't shoot a gun or a bow and arrow. And I never learned to swim. Emmeline can swim like a fish," added Audrey.

"Now *that* is something I should like to see," William admitted, causing both young ladies to blush.

"We should rejoin the others," said Charles, determined to steer them to safe waters again.

He offered his arm to Audrey, but he made no effort to engage her in conversation. As they strolled across the lush lawns, he allowed his mind to wander, wondering how things were going at the restaurant without his presence the entire day and evening.

"Have you decided where we shall picnic tomorrow?" asked Audrey finally, reminding him of her existence.

"Yes, my servants will go and set up tables in the morning. It's a lovely setting, green grass right up to the Thames and some trees for shade. At first, my grandmother refused to go; she thinks dining al fresco is barbaric."

"I think it is wonderful," said Audrey. "I love being out of doors. So is she not going?"

"Yes, she is. I promised her there would be tables for dining, so she grudgingly agreed to honor us with her presence. She wanted to know if your Miss Riggs would be there; my grandmother thinks very highly of her. Say she has brains and bottom."

Audrey laughed, saying, "I don't think our prim, proper Riggs would like to know it was put quite that way, but she is very firm in her convictions." Turning to a less pleasant topic, Audrey asked, "Are you still having the picnic catered by Chez Canard?"

Charles looked startled; he had forgotten having mentioned that to her. "Yes, I thought we would try that. Everyone says the food there is wonderful."

"So I understand," said Audrey. "I shall have to ask Uncle Gilbert to take us there one evening."

"I would be delighted to take you, Audrey." Charles smiled down at her as he wondered why he would make such a dangerous offer, allowing his two worlds to collide.

Audrey, however, brightened; she had hit upon the right thing. Though she couldn't understand what had led him to do something so odd as to go into trade, she did not condemn him. And he was so very proud of his restaurant. If it weren't for Colette, Audrey would simply confess to him that she knew all about his wager with Sir William and his avocation as a chef. But there was Colette, always between them, and Audrey remained silent.

They continued their amble through the gardens,

Audrey almost losing herself in the beauty of the flowers.

"I love the spring when everything starts to grow," she said. "I can close my eyes and think I am home again."

"You love the country, don't you?" commented Charles.

Suddenly, a disturbing thought crossed her mind, and Audrey asked anxiously, "Where are we going to live after we are married, Charles?"

Caught by surprise, he laughed. "Where do you want to live? So long as you don't say Drake's tomb, I will be happy."

"No, not unless we had a great deal of work done on it. But do you not want to live in the country?" she asked.

"I hadn't considered, really. I have been living in town, mainly to escape from my grandmother," he said with an exaggerated shiver. "And though I am not truly accustomed to country living, Audrey, I wouldn't expect to spend my entire life in town. That would be terribly confining. And when we have children"—he stopped and took her hands in his; she blushed, unable to meet his eyes—"then we would probably be much happier in the country, don't you think?"

"Yes, I know I would be," she replied, smiling sweetly at this man she loved. She had been so afraid he would insist they live forever in town. Not only did she love the country, she wasn't sure she could feel "safe" if Colette were always nearby.

"You know, Audrey, I am not a beast. Even if I

wanted to live in town, I would not do so if it made you unhappy."

"That is very considerate of you, Charles."

"There are many things we have yet to discuss," he said, taking her by the hand and strolling back into the garden, away from the crowd assembled for the supper buffet under the striped marquee.

"For instance, do you prefer coffee or tea in the morning?" he asked, frowning seriously and causing Audrey to laugh.

Audrey could not have been happier as the afternoon turned to evening. Charles was completely at ease, keeping her entertained with his witty comments and complete devotion. She found it difficult to believe that she had a rival for him. For whole minutes, she would forget about Colette and the restaurant. Then she would detect a hint of distraction and wonder if he were thinking of the sultry French beauty.

"Come with me to the house," said Emmeline, pulling Audrey to her feet. "I want to fix my hair before the dancing begins."

"We shall wait for you here," called Charles.

When they were alone, William studied his friend for a moment before commenting, "You and Miss Langston seem to be getting on famously tonight."

"Audrey is such a gentle person. I can't imagine her ever cutting up sharp over anything. I am really very fortunate to have won her."

"So you think she won't force you to sell the restaurant?"

"I don't think so. She is very open-minded for a female," said Charles.

"It's good to know you're so much in love with her," drawled William.

"Bah, what does love have to do with it? We are eminently suitable. I must admit, I toyed with the idea of Colette, a snug little house, and . . . But that would have been terribly awkward."

"You know, Charles, I ought to plant you a facer, but you're such a pompous nodcock, you probably wouldn't even know why I did it!" said William, rising and striding away.

"Devil take him," grumbled Charles.

His old friend was so head over heels in love with Emmeline Kelsey, he thought everyone should be in like case. But, Charles thought defensively, it was a rare occasion when love, marriage, and practicality could all merge into one. If it had for William, then that was all to the good!

As for him and Audrey, their marriage was for convenience and practicality; they should count themselves lucky that they were even fond of each other! They had mutual respect, and perhaps one day, this would lead them to friendship. It was all he hoped for.

When Audrey returned, she had swept her hair up to her crown, allowing curls to cascade off it in soft ringlets. Instead of being coolly elegant, she looked like a wood nymph, yielding and vulnerable. She smiled at him, tilting her head at a very fetching angle, and Charles felt a surge of desire course through his veins; the feeling took him by surprise, and he forgot to be gallant, to let her know how beautiful he found her at that moment. Audrey hid her disappointment and turned to face the marquee where people were pairing off for the first dance.

"A quadrille," he said, lightly touching her elbow. "Do you want to join them? I see Will and your cousin are already entering the fray."

"The fray? Well, if you would rather not," murmured Audrey, reading into his choice of words an antipathy for the quadrille, possibly for the whole affair.

"I didn't say that," remarked Charles. "Of course I want to dance."

His defensive manner irritated Audrey. She was quite willing to become a temptress to win his affection, but she was unprepared to coddle his every changing whim. Either he was so fatuous that he had no idea of the pain his vacillating manner caused her, or he callously didn't care!

"Very well," she said slowly, and allowed him to lead her to the temporary flooring under the huge striped tent.

They joined three other couples in making up a square. Audrey and the other ladies curtseyed, the gentlemen bowed, and the dance began. Charles's gloved hand clasped hers, and he smiled down at her before the movements of the dance separated them.

Audrey ground her teeth. How dare he! Did he think that boyish smile could make up for his lack of warmth for her? If only . . .

They came together again, and she took his hand, promising herself that she would not feel the usual rush of emotion at his touch. But it was exactly like all the other times. She fixed a polite smile on her face, hoping she wouldn't convey to him this overwhelming love she had for him. It would be too humiliating, knowing it was not reciprocated.

"You are very quiet, my dear," said Charles.

"I am a little tired," she lied.

"If you want to go home . . ."

"No, I will be fine. I wouldn't wish to spoil the evening for everyone else," said Audrey.

"I don't care about everyone else," said Charles, pressing her hand tightly.

The dance separated them once again so Audrey was saved from having to respond. If only she hadn't fallen in love with him so deeply. She thought she could be content with their marriage if she didn't love him so much. Or, if he loved her.

Her clenched jaw aching from the strain of refinement, Audrey made it through the dance, and the ones that followed. When the small orchestra struck up a waltz, she became suddenly too weary to dance. If Charles noticed this aberration, he said nothing.

By the time the evening was wearing itself out, Audrey had a raging headache and wished only for her bed. All the ladies, even the outspoken dowager, were very quiet on the way back to town, and goodbyes were accomplished swiftly.

Audrey, confessing to Riggs that her head was pounding, accepted an offer of a dose of laudanum. The small quantity brought her the repose and escape she so desperately needed.

Emmeline entered her room just as she was drifting off to sleep.

"Aude, are you awake?"

"No, Emmeline. I am asleep, or almost asleep," mumbled Audrey, wishing for once her cousin would go away.

"Oh, I wanted to talk to you."

Audrey forced her eyes open, and raised up on one elbow. "What is it, dear?" she said.

Emmeline was not her usual bubbly self. She sat on the foot of the bed and said quietly, "I am in love with William, Audrey."

"I thought you had some news for me," said Audrey, chuckling.

"I think I made a terrible mistake, though."

"What have you done?" Audrey sat up straight, every wicked possibility running through her head. Emmeline was impetuous, but surely . . .

"Yes. I . . . I told William I loved him."

Audrey laughed. "Is that all?"

"What do you mean, is that all? I should have waited until he spoke to me first! He will probably run as fast and as far as his legs will carry him!" Emmeline sniffed.

"I don't think so. William may have been surprised that you were so . . . forthcoming, but he is every bit as much in love with you as you are with him, mark my words."

"Audrey, you can't *know* that," said Emmeline hopefully.

The laudanum was having its effect on her, and her eyes drooped closed, but she whispered, "I do know, just as I know I love Charles despite the fact that he doesn't love me."

"Audrey, I don't believe that. Charles is very fond of you. Perhaps you should simply tell him you are in love with him," said Emmeline. Silence followed this suggestion, and she saw that Audrey was sound asleep. Blowing out the candles, she padded silently from the chamber.

Charles found his own form of oblivion, settling onto the soft leather sofa in his study with a decanter of brandy at his elbow which he steadily depleted until the sky was turning a pale gray.

Audrey was driving him mad! Just when he thought his courtship was progressing nicely, she withdrew from him. He cursed her for being a vexatious female, but then relented. This was an awkward business, agreeing to tie oneself to a complete stranger for life.

Still, Charles felt an instinctive affinity for Audrey. She was quiet and competent. She was a beauty, too. That should be enough, his mind chided.

But it wasn't. He yearned for a woman to love him the way he loved her. Frowning, Charles set aside his glass.

Do you love her? he asked himself.

He shook his head; it was a question he simply couldn't answer. He had never been in love; he had enjoyed alliances with a number of females, but there had never been a question of love.

So, what do you know of love? he demanded ruthlessly.

The clock over the mantel chimed six times, and he rang for coffee. He had accomplished nothing by sitting idle all night. The least he could do was go to the restaurant and make certain all was in readiness for his picnic that afternoon.

Afterward, with a few hours' sleep, he would be ready to face Audrey and his awkward dilemma once again.

Nine

"No, Papa, you must stay here and oversee the kitchen. Henry can very well look after the dining room. I will go to this picnic and serve along with Thomas."

"If you say so, my dear. But you must warn Thomas again; he must make no personal comment to the earl," said Rimbeau. "I dislike all this secrecy. Too often of late, there have been questions about the owner's true identity. Anyone could sell this information to a newspaper and ruin, not only the earl's social standing, but all of us professionally."

"I know. I think, however, that his lordship will soon realize there is no need for such secrecy," said Colette confidently.

Her father demanded sharply, "What do you mean, Colette? You are not going to do anything—"

"I will do nothing. It is the earl who will do something. Just watch and see, Papa," said the girl, smoothing her dress seductively as she thought of her plans for the earl.

"Colette! I forbid you—"

"Papa, you cannot forbid me anything. What we

have here," she said, her arms sweeping widely to indicate the entire building, "this is all my doing. You would have remained in that tiny inn until you died."

"What was so wrong with our inn?"

"Nothing, Papa," said Colette softly. "The inn was fine, but I want much, much more. And I intend to have it," she said firmly.

"Just don't . . . Now, who could that be so early in the morning?" he asked, going to the kitchen door. "Who's there?" he called.

"It is I."

"Oh, my lord," said Rimbeau, turning the lock and standing aside to allow Charles to enter. "Good morning, my lord. You are very early. No one else has arrived yet."

"I know. I just wanted to make sure . . . Oh, Colette, you're here as well."

"Yes, my lord. I, too, wanted to be certain everything would be ready for your picnic."

"You work too hard," said Charles. He watched as she crossed the room, her hips swaying gently, her pace calculated to cause a man to forget himself. With a start of surprise, Charles realized he felt nothing—no desire, no interest.

The surprise left him speechless. Here he was, a beautiful girl obviously flirting with him, and he felt no desire. Yet his senses now quickened whenever Audrey entered his sphere of vision.

Colette's father disappeared into the larder, and she said softly, "I missed you yesterday, my lord. It was the first time you did not at least come by to check on us."

"I was rather busy, Colette. And I knew, of course, that everything was safe in your competent hands."

"Thank you, *Charles,*" she replied boldly, glancing up at him through long black lashes. Her father entered the kitchen again, and she said matter-of-factly, "The tables and chairs are there, waiting to be loaded into the wagon. Those boxes contain the plate and china."

"All we need now is the food," quipped Charles. "I think I shall prepare a strawberry trifle. I will make the custard and arrange it, if you will make the syllabub, Rimbeau."

"But of course," said the older man proudly.

Charles went into the larder and found the ingredients for the custard—eggs, milk, and some isinglass. When he returned to the kitchen, Rimbeau had set a heavy pan on the stove and was stirring up the fire.

Charles dissolved the isinglass in some of the milk and slowly added the egg yolks, stirring it over the flame so it could thicken.

The activity in the kitchen increased as some of the lower chefs arrived for the day. Amid the hubbub of all this, Charles's mind drifted back to Audrey and the previous night when she had been so fickle. He sighed and stirred, wondering why women had to be so difficult. Couldn't they be more decisive, like men?

"The custard! Mr. Brown!" shouted Randall.

"Damn and blast!" muttered Charles, yanking the burnt concoction off the stove, burning his hand as it sloshed over the top of the pan.

"See to your hand, sir," said Randall. "I'll wash this."

"Thank you, Randall. I don't know where my mind was."

Colette appeared with some butter, pulling his hand toward her to rub the soothing balm on the tender skin.

"You must be more careful, Charles," she whispered.

"Yes, I will in the future," said Charles. "Thank you," he added. "I have had little rest. I think I shall go home until time for the picnic. Tell your father to make whatever he will. I'm sure he will know what to do."

"Very well. I will see you at the picnic."

Charles frowned. "You are going to be there?"

"You need someone to wait on you and your friends," said Colette. "Thomas will be assisting me."

"Uh, Colette, I don't know if that would be wise." Charles suddenly realized he had no desire to be near her, especially when Audrey would be by his side. If Audrey were to discover . . .

For the first time, he felt uneasy about owning Chez Canard. Before his betrothal to Audrey, if he had been discovered, he wouldn't have cared very much, except for the sake of his wager with William. But the thought of Audrey being involved made him decidedly uncomfortable. What would she do if she discovered the truth? Would she call off their betrothal? The idea made him blanch.

"But, my lord," Colette was saying, "there is no

one else we can spare. Do not worry; I will see to it
that your guests are content."

Charles acquiesced; she had been too efficient in
the past to quibble over this picnic. She knew of his
wish to remain anonymous; she would be competent
and discreet, and she would see to it that Thomas
was the same.

"We shall serve at four o'clock, correct, my lord?"
she asked, making notes on a sheet of paper, her
capable manner setting his mind at ease.

"Yes, and you know the location so you can arrive
early and have everything in readiness," he said.

"You can depend on me, my lord," said Colette.

"And I do," said Charles, settling his hat on his
head and bidding them farewell.

Audrey's smooth brow wrinkled with indecision. "I
just can't decide, Millie. Which gown should I wear?"

"Well, miss, the green is ever so pretty, and since
you will be outdoors, you will look as fresh as the
grass."

Audrey kept her mirth hidden and commented,
"Ah, but do I want to look like grass? What of the
blue gown?"

"It's very pretty, miss, and with that bodice, all the
gentlemen will be vying for a seat by your side."

Audrey shook her head and smiled. "Then it had
best be the green. I have had quite enough of gentlemen and their strange habits."

"Yes, miss," said the abigail, shaking her head at
her mistress's odd notions.

For her part, Audrey vowed that she was finished playing games with Charles. She might be bound by the betrothal, but she would not be bound by her love. If he came to love her over time, then well and good. If not, she would simply have to resign herself to a marriage of expedience.

Such a thought was very lowering and frustrating for a young woman who was accustomed to getting her own way, to making things turn out the way she wanted them to evolve. But Audrey knew she could not control Charles or his emotions, and if he could not love her, then she would learn to live with it.

"The carriage is at the door, Audrey," said Emmeline, pausing by her cousin's room as she hurried toward the stairs.

"Don't you look pretty!" said Audrey. "And so tall and slender!"

Emmeline gave her throaty laugh. "You are a flatterer. Trying to take my mind off what I told William last night?" she asked.

"What in the world are you talking about?" Audrey tied on her straw bonnet. "What has William to do with it, except that he is bound to be bewitched by your costume."

Grinning, Emmeline tripped across the room to look at her image one more time. "Well, I do think the striped spencer is very becoming. And I like the pink. I always thought pink an insipid color, but now I find it quite becoming."

"That is because it is rose, not pink," said Audrey. "Now, if you are finished admiring yourself, we really must be going."

"I'm coming," said Emmeline, following Audrey out of the room. "William says we are in for a real treat. He says Charles's food is spectacular."

"Shhh! We mustn't refer to it as Charles's food," warned Audrey. "We are not supposed to know about his aberration."

Emmeline's giggles burst into loud laughter as they descended the stairs and saw Charles waiting in the hall.

"Aberration," she whispered in choked accents. "Audrey, it is too bad of you."

"Shhh! Behave yourself!" Audrey admonished. "Good afternoon, Middlehurst. Is Sir William with you?"

So it is going to be "Middlehurst" today, thought Charles. "William said he would meet us there. The other ladies are already in the carriage, so if you are ready?"

"Of course, let us go. I have been looking forward to this afternoon for a week," said Audrey formally.

"As have I," Charles replied, grinning at her as she moved past him. He would be just as punctilious as she!

Charles had taken care of the smallest detail for the picnic. There were six large round tables set up, each with sparkling white cloths. On two were silver platters with thinly sliced meats and cheeses. Spilling out of serving bowls were a variety of fruits and vegetables. There were also roasted pheasant and dilled potatoes and iced champagne, and in the center of the second table was a beautiful strawberry trifle surrounded by delicate pastries.

The other tables were set for dining with the finest china, silver, and crystal. For anyone who preferred sitting on the ground, colorful blankets dotted the green grass. Beyond the array of food, the Thames progressed lazily along its way. Lord Asherton was already there, rowing a Miss Hampton in a small boat. Mr. Parnell and Lady Caroline were playing a spirited game of croquet. There was a gentle breeze, and the sun shone happily.

"It is beautiful," said Emmeline, hopping to the ground and hurrying toward Sir William, who took both her hands in his and led her toward the water's edge.

"I hope those chairs under the trees over there are comfortable," said Lady Middlehurst, descending stiffly from the carriage.

"They are, Grandmother. Allow me to escort you."

"No, no, you run along. Miss Riggs and Mrs. Kelsey will help me."

"Of course, my lady," said Riggs, offering her arm to the dowager countess.

"You must try a taste of this," said Charles, pointing to the trifle as he escorted Audrey past the heavily laden tables. Colette paused, watching.

"It looks delicious, Charles," said Audrey, lifting her chin, her blue eyes issuing a silent challenge to the French girl.

Charles, unaware of the struggle, asked, "Audrey, what would you like to do first? Shall we join Parnell and Lady Caroline at croquet? Or Perhaps a boat ride is more to your liking."

"No, Charles, I don't care for the water, never having learned to swim," said Audrey.

"But I thought you could swim like a fish," he teased, then added, "Ah, no, that was your cousin, was it not?"

"Yes, Emmeline almost drowned once, so her father insisted she learn to swim."

"But what about croquet? Would you . . . ?" Charles frowned, looking over Audrey's shoulder at Colette. "Excuse me one moment, my dear. There must be some problem with the food."

Charles hurried toward Colette, who gave Audrey a smirk before smiling broadly at her quarry. Turning, Audrey crossed the green lawn and joined her aunt under the trees. Out of the corner of her eye, she watched Charles and her rival.

He didn't appear to be enjoying their conversation, thought Audrey, trying not to gloat, but not succeeding very well. Then Colette stalked away, leaving Charles to glare after her before deciding to follow her. They stopped again beside the wagon.

"She is just a waitress, my dear," said the dowager countess quietly. "Not worthy of your notice."

"Who?" intoned Audrey haughtily.

"That's the spirit!" cackled the older woman.

"Lady Middlehurst, I was just remarking to Riggs here that I would like to go to Paris. I was wondering, have you ever been to Paris?" asked Aunt Patricia, intervening opportunely.

"Many years ago, but it was not pleasant. There was too much unrest. I remember . . ."

Audrey tuned out the remainder of the conversation. She craned her neck to find Charles and Colette, but they had disappeared. Rising, she remarked casually that she wanted to see the water, and wandered away.

Privately, she wished she could take Charles and throttle him! Though she promised herself she would not seek him out, her eyes discovered him again. He appeared to be in a hot debate with Colette. Her face had lost its smirk completely, and she appeared agitated. So much the better! thought Audrey smugly.

"Audrey, would you like to go for a boat ride?" called Emmeline from the edge of the water.

Audrey shook her head vehemently.

Miss Hampton, a vapid girl of eighteen, hung on Lord Asherton's arm and lisped, "You really thould go, Mith Langthon. It ith ever tho much fun."

Audrey cringed, but she looked back one last time and saw Colette's hand stroke Charles's jaw.

The intimate gesture induced her to lie boldly. "Yes, I would enjoy that above all things."

Sir William helped her step into the small vessel and steadied it while she sat down on one of the wooden benches.

Emmeline pretended to climb in and stopped, saying, "William, this is too small for three people. I'll wait here; we can go out later."

"No, no," said Audrey, starting to rise, but the boat rocked so, she sat back down quickly.

"No, Aude, I insist. William would love to, wouldn't you, William?" Emmeline added, winking at him.

"Of course I would. Audrey, you just stay put while I shove us off." William and Emmeline exchanged a few whispered words, and he nodded.

Audrey, eyeing the water nervously, missed all of Sir William's and Emmeline's winks. If she hadn't, she would have known immediately that something was afoot. As it was, Sir William rowed them steadily to the middle of the river. Audrey released her hold on the bench long enough to manage a tiny wave to Lord Asherton, his silly companion, and Emmeline.

"You don't like the water very much, do you, Miss Langston?" commented Sir William.

"No," she said with a nervous laugh. "However could you tell?"

"You don't seem to be enjoying yourself," said the large man gently. "You know, Charles isn't really a nodcock; it's just that sometimes, he is so naive."

"A naive, thirty-one-year-old veteran of Spain and Portugal?" she drawled.

"You give Charles, or for that matter many of us old soldiers, a battle to fight, and we know exactly what is to be done. But this love business . . . That's an entirely different matter. Most of us would rather face Napoleon's finest than flirt with love."

"You are a very persuasive man, Sir William."

"I just happen to know how my friend thinks. Thought that way myself before I met your cousin Emmeline." William looked up, suddenly evincing a great interest in the sky.

"What kind of clouds are those?" he asked.

Audrey looked up as well and therefore missed the large rock William pushed overboard, quickly followed by one of the oars.

"Damn! Er, pardon, Miss Langston. I dropped an oar," said William, leaning over, his weight causing the boat to tip precariously.

"Well, can't you row with only one?" asked Audrey, her grip tightening.

"No, that's not possible. I think I can reach it," said Sir William, leaning out even farther. Suddenly, there was a splash, and he disappeared over the side of the boat.

Audrey screamed and stood up; the boat rocked wildly. She collapsed onto the bench again, her face white with fear.

"Help! Help!" she screamed with all her might.

The guests rushed to the shore, shouting and asking questions. Audrey looked over the edge of the boat, twisting as far as she could, but she saw no sign of William.

Frantic now, she picked up the remaining oar and attempted to maneuver the boat for a better view.

"Audrey, sit still!" screamed Charles from the shore, while Asherton helped him remove his boots.

In that moment, everything became crystal clear. He didn't care about Chez Canard, cooking, or anything else if it did not include Audrey. Why had that custard burned? It was not because he was tired; that had never made any difference before. He had been thinking of Audrey. He loved her! And unless he hurried, he might lose her forever. Panic made him fumble with the buttons of his coat as he removed it.

"I can't find William, Charles!" she wailed.

Then she frowned, noticing the odd piece of rope hanging over the side of the boat. Crawling forward, she yanked on it; there was some weight on the end. Though horrified lest she discover Sir William hanging from it, nevertheless, she began hauling it on board, not noticing that the small boat was once again floating down the river. As she tugged on the rope, she soon saw a large rock rising to the surface; when she gave the rope a final, mighty yank, the rock slipped off the rope, and the boat shot forward.

"What in the world?" she said, not hearing the splash as Charles entered the cold water. "Charles, help me!" she screamed.

William, jumping up from the bushes where he was hiding on the other side of the river, dove into the water, but after a few strokes, he began treading water, having realized rescue was hopeless from his vantage point.

With a curse, Charles sloshed back on shore and ran to where the horses were tethered. He grabbed the reins of Lord Asherton's gelding. Emmeline restrained him, her face white with fear.

"We didn't mean for this to happen, Charles!"

"We?" he snarled. He looked across the river as he heard William yelling from the far bank. He would deal with him later. Grabbing a horse's mane, he swung up on its bare back, hanging on tightly as the beast sprung forward.

Charles tried to call to Audrey, but his voice failed him, so choked was he with fear. Cantering along the bank, he watched her panic grow and willed her to remain still. He knew the river fairly well and was aware that there were shallows not far ahead, if only he could reach her before she panicked completely.

Clearing his throat, he shouted, "Be still; I'll save you!" He kicked at the horse's sides with his stockinged heels, passing Audrey. Reaching the shallow waters, he jumped to the ground and waded toward the center, only losing his footing when he reached the middle.

He followed Audrey's progress by the sound of her cries for help. She had lost track of him and was too frightened to turn and see him. The water was deeper in the center, and Charles shouted to attract her attention before he dove into it.

"Charles!" screamed Audrey, thinking he, too, would be lost. Then a hand reached out to steady the boat, slowing its progress until it almost stopped. Charles's head appeared, and Audrey, forgetting his instructions to sit still, stood up and leaned toward him, capsizing the tiny craft and landing in the water on top of Charles.

She grabbed his head, scrambling to find the surface, trying to scream and swallowing water instead. Charles tried to steady her, but she was like a wild woman, dragging him down time and again. Finally their struggles brought them back to the shallow side, and Charles found a firm hold on her waist and thrust her into the air.

"Stand up, Audrey! Stand up!" he shouted, gasping for air and laughing at her.

Quieting suddenly, Audrey found her footing. She

raised a hand to slap him, but he caught it easily. Capturing her hands, he kissed her soundly.

Coughing, Audrey threw her arms around his neck, her lips seeking his. It was as if the heavens had burst into flames; Audrey returned Charles's kisses with wild abandon. Picking her up, he staggered under the weight of her garments, but neither wanted to release the other, and they made it to shore, his head bent to hers, his lips tasting her passion. They fell onto the green grass, still wrapped in each other's arms.

Charles pushed the wet hair from her face and gazed into her eyes.

"Are you all right?" he asked.

"Yes, but Sir William—"

"He's fine, though he may not be when I get finished with him," said Charles.

He smiled then and pulled her against his chest. "You are never getting into another boat—ever," he whispered after tenderly kissing her lips.

Nodding vigorously, Audrey propped herself up on her elbows, her eyes straying to his lips with longing. Reading her thoughts, Charles smiled, leaning closer. She closed her eyes in anticipation.

"You are so very beautiful, Audrey," he whispered, his lips grazing hers.

One hand encircled her waist while the other slipped under her neck. Slowly, he kissed her forehead, her eyes, her nose, and finally, lingeringly, her lips. Audrey's arms pulled him close, and she pressed against his hard body.

After a few moments, Charles pushed away, smiling

and murmuring, "My dearest girl," before Audrey wound her fingers in his wet hair and pulled his mouth back down to hers.

"Halloo! Charles!" called several unwelcome voices.

Charles sat up hurriedly, rising and turning to help Audrey to her feet.

"Oh, there you are! We found William," said Parnell. "Most extraordinary story."

The others gathered around, waiting for Charles to tell his end of the yarn. Colette had followed, too, but she hung back, watching in silence.

"As you can see, we all survived," Charles started. He reached for Audrey's hand, refusing to release her until they were back at the picnic site.

Asherton discovered, in the boot of his carriage, a pair of old trousers for Charles. William, having planned for this disaster with Emmeline, had a spare suit of clothes, and he also shared with Charles.

Charles placed his dry coat around Audrey's shaking shoulders before turning to glare at Emmeline and William, his mouth white with anger. Audrey was quite beyond repair, wet from the skin out and chilled to the bone. She sneezed, and Riggs bundled her into the carriage for the ride back to town.

Charles, leaning close at the window, squeezed her hand, and whispered softly, "I will call on you later." He kissed her fingertips before stepping back and signaling the driver to spring 'em.

Audrey's heart skipped a beat, and she watched him from the window until they were almost to the road. Sitting back, she said a little prayer of thanksgiving for Sir William and Emmeline and their hare-brained plan to have Charles rescue her. The end results had been nothing short of stupendous!

"A word with you, William," growled Charles when the carriage was away.

"Now, Charles, I—"

That was as far as he got; Charles's fist crashed into William's jaw, sending him reeling. Emmeline rushed forward, cradling William's head in her lap.

"You bacon-brained clodpole! If you ever do anything to endanger Audrey again, I . . . I shall call you out!" Whirling away, he tripped over Colette who was at his elbow.

"I am sorry, my lord. If I could just have a word with you. We should have served half an hour ago. I fear the hot dishes will not be up to your usual standards," she said.

"I don't care what the deuce it tastes like. Serve the bloody food so we can get away from here!" Charles snarled, stalking away to the table where his grandmother was seated with Audrey's aunt. He dropped onto a chair, staring off at nothing.

"I was just saying to Mrs. Kelsey, Charles, that this has been the most amusing picnic I have ever attended!" said his grandmother.

Charles ignored her.

"Was all of this entertainment planned?" she asked.

Charles swiveled on the seat and, leaning both elbows on the table so that his face was close to hers, drawled with awful sarcasm, "Yes, Grandmother. It was all part of my grand scheme to entertain you! Audrey almost drowning—what a lark!"

"No need to get peevish, my boy. You must be hungry. I'll ask that nice French girl to fix you a plate."

Charles's eyes almost popped out of his head. He pushed away from the table and stood over her.

"Devil take you, madam. You know, don't you?"

"Charles, I am an old woman; you must realize I am not very conversant in the ways of modern London."

"You *do* know." He turned and backed away from the table. "You know all about Chez Canard. But how?"

"Lord Middlehurst, perhaps you should sit down. You are very flushed," said Audrey's aunt.

The others began to gather around them. Charles was still shaking his head as though trying to clear it of a great fog.

"Charles, remember where you are," warned William. "Remember the wager."

"The devil take that deuced wager! You think I care about the money?"

"Charles, now is not the time," said William.

"Charles, you are making a spectacle of yourself. William, why don't you take my grandson home? I believe this afternoon has been too much of a shock for him, almost losing his beloved Audrey. Now, don't be afraid," she said to William. "I'm sure he has recovered from his fit of temper with you."

"Fit of temper?" murmured Charles, still eyeing his grandmother with incredulity and awe. Then he grinned and gave a shout of laughter, causing his friends and family to back away, all except William and the dowager countess.

"Come on, Charles, let's go back to town. Asherton, Parnell, you'll bake care of things here?"

Both gentlemen nodded, and two grooms hurried to harness Sir William's pair to his curricle.

When they had been on the road for several minutes, Charles broke his distracted silence.

"That woman is a sorceress," he said. "How the devil did she know?"

"The servants?" offered William.

Charles shook his head. "They have never worked for her. Remember, she hasn't come to town in ten or fifteen years."

"Maybe she is a witch," said William. "She certainly makes me want to stay out of the range of her spells," he said with a shiver.

"I don't think there is a limit to her 'range,' William. She is omnipotent! God help us all!" he added.

"You know, I wonder why I remain your friend. I could avoid her completely if I avoided you."

"Too late. She knows too much about you," said Charles with a sardonic laugh.

"So what will you do now?" asked William.

"About the restaurant? I haven't decided yet."

"Perhaps you can sell it to make enough money to pay me my winnings." William laughed.

He lifted his eyes in surprise when Charles, after a moment of consideration, said, "Perhaps I should."

Ten

Wrapped in shawls, Audrey waited for Charles to call, her anger and disappointment multiplying with each chime of the clock. Millie had insisted her mistress take a steaming bath when she returned, still soaking wet and sneezing. Dressed in flannel nightrail, Audrey had sat by the fire, its warmth drying her long curls.

Now, evening had fallen, her hair had dried completely, and still she waited for Charles. She felt like a quiz, one of those strange children's toys, pulled up one moment toward happy memories and the next propelled down into misery.

Where is he? she demanded of herself, a question she knew she could not answer. All she could do was try to ignore the evil inner demon who whispered, "It is Tuesday; he is at the restaurant with Colette."

Emmeline and Sir William had gone to a rout with Riggs along to chaperon. Her aunt was resting, and her uncle had gone to his club. There was no one to talk to, no one to commiserate with.

She had thought, had hoped, that Charles would come to her. Had he not felt the same explosion of desire that she had that afternoon when they lay together, dripping wet, their silent lips speaking honestly to each other for the very first time? Surely he had!

Audrey heard a carriage pull up to the house a short time after midnight. Emmeline, laughing, invited Sir William inside to share the tea tray. Audrey hastened to her bed, blowing out the candle and pulling up the coverlet before her cousin's inevitable entrance.

"Audrey?" Emmeline whispered, listening for some response. When there was none, she backed out the door, humming happily as she returned to her William.

Audrey tried not to be petty and begrudge her cousin a smooth road to love. She vowed that she wanted no one else to suffer as she had. Still, it would all have been worth it if only Charles had called!

Audrey awoke late the next morning, feeling groggy instead of rested. When she saw the time, she jumped out of bed. Sometime in the middle of the night, she had made the decision to confront Charles about the restaurant, and more to the point, about Colette. With this in mind, she dressed carefully in her most becoming carriage dress, telling Millie to fetch a cloak as she was to accompany her mistress on an important errand.

Mission is the more appropriate word, thought Audrey, marching out the door and down the front steps. It was still too early for a call, but she wanted to strike before she lost her nerve.

She met her first obstacle in the form of Duncan, Charles's competent butler.

"I insist that you take me to his lordship," she reiterated firmly. When he again denied her, she intoned regally, "Do you know who I am?"

"Certainly, Miss Langston. I realize you are his lordship's betrothed, but I cannot take you to him when he has already gone out for the day."

Audrey frowned, pursing her lips.

The butler brightened. "I could, however, inquire as to her ladyship's presence."

"Yes, yes. Please do so at once," said Audrey.

"If you would be so good as to step this way, Miss Langston. I shall ascertain whether her ladyship is at home."

"Thank you, Duncan."

Audrey looked around the cozy drawing room where she and Charles had sparred over fashion. Smiling, she didn't hear the door open.

"Have you misplaced my wayward grandson?" asked the dowager countess, smiling at her visitor.

"I. . . ." Audrey pulled out her handkerchief to combat the sudden flow of tears.

"Here now, my dear. Join me," said the countess, taking a seat on the sofa.

Audrey obliged her, sniffing a few times before she regained her composure.

"You mustn't worry about Charles. I know he is doing the right thing."

"What might that be?" asked Audrey.

"It might be any number of things. But I know Charles. He is very conscientious, but very slow and methodical."

"He never called last night," said Audrey, her brow knitted with worry.

The countess patted her hand. "He is a gudgeon at times, is he not? Reminds me of my late husband in that. But you don't care to hear about my other Charles," added the countess, laughingly recognizing the fact that Audrey was failing miserably at trying to appear interested in family history.

"Do you know where I may find Charles, my lady?"

"I couldn't say; I have my ideas, but I think divulging them would only make matters between you worse."

"Is he at the restaurant?" asked Audrey, lifting her eyes to meet the countess's sharp gaze.

"So, you do know. I underestimated you, my dear."

"But you didn't answer my question," said Audrey, her sudden composure chilling to behold.

"Yes, my dear, I think he must be. Would you like me to accompany you there?" asked the dowager.

Audrey shook her head and the countess asked sensibly, "Do you have your carriage? No? Then let me send you in one of Charles's. Wait here."

Audrey stood back and allowed Charles's footman to knock on the restaurant's heavy front doors. When there was no answer, she told him to return to the carriage and marched around the side of the building, her maid doggedly on her heels.

She beat a loud tattoo on the side door, the one Charles had slipped through that day when she had spied on him. When no one answered immediately, she tried the door, which gave easily as she turned the handle.

Stepping inside, she met a thin, dark man dressed in a chef's apron.

"May I be of service, madam?" he asked, his polite tones soothing Audrey's burst of apprehension.

"I . . . I wish to see Mr. Brown."

"I am sorry, madam. Mr. Brown is with someone at the moment. If you would care to wait?"

"Yes, thank you, I would."

"Right this way."

Audrey found herself in a large, airy kitchen. Another man was busy kneading bread, but otherwise, it was empty. The first man indicated a chair across from a dark door.

"I'm sorry you have to wait in the kitchen, madam, but that is Mr. Brown's office."

"I don't mind," said Audrey, fuming inwardly while she kept her polite mask firmly in place.

So Charles was "with someone." She seethed. One day he was rescuing her and making love to her on the grass and the next he was romancing some French . . .

Fifteen minutes passed, and Audrey was almost ready to burst through the office door when it opened.

Colette appeared, gazing back toward Charles, presumably with stars in her eyes.

"Thank you, my lord," she said before turning and

floating out of the kitchen, not even noticing Audrey's presence.

Audrey, however, took in each minute detail of the girl's costume and demeanor. With a sinking spirit, she thought they must be very thick indeed for Colette to be closeted with him in his office.

But it was Charles in there, her Charles. She stiffened her spine and rose, marching toward the closed door.

Thrusting it open, Audrey glared at Charles who was standing behind his desk, shuffling through some papers as if he had not just been making love to the French girl!

"Audrey! What a—" he began.

"Do not try to gammon me," she snapped, slamming the door. "I am here to give you an ultimatum. If you are going to wed me, you will sell this cursed restaurant and vow never to see that Colette person again! Furthermore, you will marry me as soon as a special license may be obtained. And you will promise me that the only person you will ever cook for again will be me!"

Grinning from ear to ear, Charles stepped around the desk, hurrying to her side. He took her hands and turned them over to kiss her palms. Audrey shivered with delight.

Then he pulled her forward, gesturing toward one of the tall-backed chairs facing the desk.

"Rimbeau, Prufrock, you have not had the privilege of meeting my fiancée. This is Miss Audrey Langston," he said proudly.

Rimbeau rose and bowed deeply before the morti-
fied girl. *"Enchanté, mademoiselle."*

"Delighted," said a short, round man with very
thick spectacles.

Still grinning in the most infuriating manner,
Charles added, "Darling, this is my solicitor, Mr. Prufrock. And you must congratulate my former em-
ployee here, Monsieur Rimbeau, Audrey. He has just
this morning purchased Chez Canard—he and his
efficient daughter Colette."

Blushing painfully, Audrey curtseyed and said,
"How do you do? My most hearty congratulations to
you and your daughter, monsieur."

"You are too kind, mademoiselle," Rimbeau said,
bowing once again before heading for the door.

Mr. Prufrock mumbled a quick farewell and hurried past the Frenchman.

Rimbeau paused to murmur, "Ah, love," before
leaving them alone.

Charles wasted no time capturing Audrey in his embrace. Even his hearty laughter did not anger her,
she was so grateful that her Charles had done as she
wished before she had even delivered her ultimatum.

"You know, Audrey, I always thought I was such a
clever fellow, but I find I am very stupid about love.
I hope you will teach me."

"I can't think of anything I would rather do with
my life, Charles. I. . . ." Audrey blushed again, and
Charles lifted her chin so he could look into her eyes.

"You . . . ?"

"I feel very foolish, Charles. I told Emmeline she
should have waited to tell William, and here I am,

about to do the same thing. But I want you to know, Charles. I want everyone to know—I love you, Charles, so very much."

"Isn't that wonderful!" he exclaimed, stealing a quick kiss before confessing, "And I love you, more than I ever thought I could love a woman. Will you be my wife, my dearest Audrey?"

"Yes, Charles, yes!" Audrey replied.

He kissed her again, then led her to the chair, and sat down, pulling her onto his lap. Their lovemaking burst into passionate embraces and kisses until Charles drew back, shifting his weight uncomfortably.

"A special license, you said?"

Audrey nodded.

"That sounds like an excellent idea." There was a rumble, and he laughed. "Are you hungry, my love?"

"It is the smells coming from the kitchen," she confessed. "I haven't eaten since . . . I don't remember when I ate last."

"Perhaps Rimbeau will let me cook up a little something, just for the two of us."

"That sounds, and smells wonderful," said Audrey, climbing off his lap.

With a leer and a very thick French accent, Charles promised, "I will whip us up a sinfully delicious luncheon—a *dîner a deux.*"

"Just for the two of us," whispered Audrey, following his lead with a sultry glance.

"Oui, oui, just for the two of us," said Charles, stealing another kiss. "But I am not sure, *mademoiselle,* if I can bear to stop kissing you long enough for you to enjoy it. I make no promises."

"Better and better," said Audrey, laughing, her eyes filled with love.

Sobering, Charles lifted her hand to his lips. "I do promise one thing, my love. There will be no other woman in my life, only you," he added, taking her in his arms again.

Epilogue

"Is he here yet?" Audrey asked, torn between anger and exasperation.

"Not yet," said Emmeline. "I sent William to look for him half an hour ago."

"Any sign?" Riggs popped her head into the antechamber at St. Paul's.

"No, I don't know what to—"

"He's here!" called Uncle Gilbert from the hall.

"Thank heavens!" whispered Audrey.

"I thought we were going to have a murder on our hands instead of a wedding," said Emmeline, helping Audrey straighten her wedding gown. "You look so beautiful."

"It's time." Rupert Langston appeared at the door. "Charles is a very lucky man," he said proudly.

"Thank you, Papa."

"For one thing, he'll never be late again with you around."

"Papa!" Audrey chided.

They followed the sound of the music. Emmeline and William were waiting at the front of the church with Charles. He was looking a little frazzled despite his elegant black coat and pantaloons. But when he saw Audrey, his face lit up with delight, his blue eyes bright and shining with love.

When she reached the altar, she whispered, "Where were you?"

"Shhh, later," he replied, turning to face the vicar.

"We are gathered. . . ."

Her mother and father cried; his grandmother gloated. Emmeline and William gazed longingly into each other's eyes over the heads of the bride and groom.

"You may kiss the bride," said the vicar.

Charles leaned down for a chaste kiss. Audrey pulled his head down for a more consummating symbol. Her mother groaned; his grandmother cackled.

When Audrey released Charles, she licked her lips and frowned.

"Syllabub?" she whispered.

"Did you think I would let this day go by without cooking up something extra special?" He laughed, taking her arm and helping her down the steps and up the aisle.

"A strawberry trifle?" she asked, shaking her head and smiling up at him.

"The very same," he said proudly.

"Charles, I don't wish to hurt your feelings, and perhaps I shouldn't tell you now, but I truly despise strawberries."

He stopped halfway up the aisle, causing the others to pull up short, too.

"You're not angry, are you?" asked Audrey hurriedly.

His shoulders started shaking, and he said lightly, "There is really so much we must discover about each other. I look forward to every day—and night—together, my love!"

About the Author

Donna Bell lives in Flower Mound, Texas, with Dennis, her husband of more than twenty-seven years. Her daughters Jamie and Tiffany have recently married, adding two wonderful sons-in-law to the family, David and Scott. Her son Stuart is a senior in high school and still lives at home.

Donna teaches high school French when she is not writing, taking care of her family, her pets, her hobbies, etc. She would like to be cloned so her double could grade all the papers and do all the housework while she props up her feet, writes, reads, and cross-stitches.

Send her e-mail at dendon@gte.net.

BOOK YOUR PLACE ON OUR WEBSITE AND MAKE THE READING CONNECTION!

We've created a customized website just for our very special readers, where you can get the inside scoop on everything that's going on with Zebra, Pinnacle and Kensington books.

When you come online, you'll have the exciting opportunity to:

- View covers of upcoming books
- Read sample chapters
- Learn about our future publishing schedule (listed by publication month *and author*)
- Find out when your favorite authors will be visiting a city near you
- Search for and order backlist books from our online catalog
- Check out author bios and background information
- Send e-mail to your favorite authors
- Meet the Kensington staff online
- Join us in weekly chats with authors, readers and other guests
- Get writing guidelines
- AND MUCH MORE!

**Visit our website at
http://www.zebrabooks.com**